ABOUT THE AUTHOR

RJ Scott lives just outside London. She has been writing since age six, when she was made to stay in at lunchtime for an infraction involving cookies and was told to write a story. Two sides of A4 about a trapped princess later, a lover of writing was born. She loves reading anything from thrillers to sci-fi to horror; however, her first real love will always be the world of romance. Her goal is to write stories with a heart of romance, a troubled road to reach happiness, and more than a hint of happily ever after.

Email:
rj@rjscott.co.uk

Webpage:
www.rjscott.co.uk

Facebook:
http://www.facebook.com/rjscotts

Twitter:
@rjscotts

STILL WATERS

A SANCTUARY STORY

RJ SCOTT

SILVER PUBLISHING
Published by Silver Publishing
Publisher of Erotic Romance

¶SILVERPUBLISHING

ISBN 978-1-61495-706-5

Still Waters

Copyright © 2012 by RJ Scott
Editor: Liz Bichmann
Cover Artist: Reese Dante

Visit Silver Publishing at https://spsilverpublishing.com

Note from the Publisher

Dear Reader,

Thank you for your purchase of this title. The authors and staff of Silver Publishing hope you enjoy this read and that we will have a long and happy association together.

Please remember that the only money authors make from writing comes from the sales of their books. If you like their work, spread the word and tell others about the books, but please refrain from copying this book in any form. Authors depend on sales and sales only to support their families.

If you see "free shares" offered or cut-rate sales of this title on ebook pirate sites, you can report the offending entry to copyright@spsilverpublishing.com.

Thank you for not pirating our titles.

Lodewyk Deysel
Publisher
Silver Publishing
http://www.spsilverpublishing.com

DEDICATION

For every single one of you who have told me you are enjoying this five book series. Thank you. Your kind words mean so much to me.

And, always for my family.

Trademarks Acknowledgement

CHAPTER 1

"Have you ever wondered how much Jake is worth? Or how much it costs every day to run this Foundation?" Nik Valentinov asked as he sat down opposite Adam Brooke.

Adam was looking around at the luxurious décor of Sanctuary Imports and Exports. He concentrated on what Nik had said, not entirely sure if the other agent was asking a rhetorical question. If other operatives were like him then he'd bet Nik had contemplated their boss's fortune at one time or another.

"Probably one hell of a lot," Adam finally offered. Leaning back in the leather chair and resting his feet on the small coffee table he closed his eyes. He wasn't being rude intentionally but his body was winding down and he really needed sleep. He should probably be considering downtime but getting caught up in the problems on the Bullen case had his juices flowing.

His last real case—the Canada safe house gig—had been a bad one. Even Sanctuary had to help hide the bad guys sometimes but not a single one of the hundred or so men and women that worked for Jake were impressed when it was their turn. Low-level drug dealer or not, the guy had been caught at a school peddling his wares to kids not much older than twelve. The 'get 'em hooked young' policy was one the scumbag clearly subscribed to. Unfortunately for Adam, his charge had been the lynchpin in a much bigger case and that was what had been deemed important. The FBI didn't have the capacity to look after the guy. Sanctuary stepped in. Adam hated it when Sanctuary stepped in to mop up FBI shit.

Three weeks with a guy who gave slimy a bad name and Adam was way past over it with the whole drug thing. He really hoped this new assignment, whatever it involved, was something he could get his teeth into. Action, cars, guns, and maybe a good beat down would rid his body of the itch of isolation with someone who thought Jerry Springer re-runs were high art.

"Did your guy get sent down?" Nik began conversationally.

Adam opened his eyes and quirked a smile. This he could handle talking about. "Yep. Heard he got max what they could give even with the deal on handing over his suppliers."

Nik grinned at this and crossed his arms over his chest. "Did you hear from Doc at all? Did the direct hit break any of his ribs?" Nik was referring to Doctor Kayden Summers getting shot in the chest at the bank vault where he and the Bullen kid were retrieving evidence. Adam had been there to spirit Beckett away before he became the subject of the late news.

"Yeah. He has access to good meds," Adam smirked. "How's Morgan?"

Nik's expression changed immediately. Adam saw pride and affection and it was a nice thing to see in another person. Nik had spent at least five minutes with his cell stuck to his ear talking to Morgan. Adam had to wonder at what they found to talk about for so long when they were together so much of the time.

Nik and Morgan had the cliché bodyguard-victim relationship that appeared to be stronger than two-by-fours joined together with a nail gun.

"He's good. He's still doing well with his art and he's not really under Sanctuary anymore." Unspoken was the 'but I look out for him anyway'. That was given. Adam hadn't actually met Morgan but he knew all the details of the case. Three weeks alone, avoiding the idiot he was guarding, gave him a lot of time for reading.

"Do you know where we're being assigned?" Adam was curious.

Nik shrugged his wide shoulders.

"Is this a double team assignment?" It was a valid question. Sanctuary operatives generally worked alone unless the case was so diverse or volatile that two were needed. The last time Adam had doubled up had been with Jennifer out of LA and it had been kind of nice to have intellectual company. Not that he was saying some of his charges weren't clever. Jeez, he'd been the one tasked with that physicist job last fall. But the last job had frazzled any and all of his remaining brain cells.

Normally, unless operatives were working together on a case, briefings were kept separate. So he assumed they were being assigned together. Despite having crossed paths with Nik at the FBI he had never worked with Nik before at Sanctuary so it should be interesting. Although he'd probably find Morgan hiding in Nik's suitcase.

"Come in guys," Jake called from

around his office door and Adam pushed himself to stand. Stretching tall he followed Nik into the large corner office overlooking downtown Albany.

"Coffee?" Jake was busying himself with the huge chrome contraption that wouldn't have looked out of place in a science fiction movie but under Jake's skilled touch it made the best coffee Adam had ever tasted. He nodded yes, as did Nik, and finally all three men sat on sofas.

Jake didn't waste any time and cut right to the chase. "As you are both very aware Sanctuary, for obvious reasons, is way in over its head with this Bullen case. Not only did we add Morgan but we now have Beckett Jamieson under our care. To complicate it further you're probably also aware I have an FBI liaison at the moment auditing our procedures and writing up channels of communication between us."

Adam searched Jake's expression for a

clue as to how the guy felt about this shadow but, ever the professional, Jake's expression was impassive.

"He is not party to all information concerning our actions on the Bullen case but on each occasion, after we got involved, the FBI have wanted first Morgan, then Beckett, back under their auspices."

Nik had moved forward in his seat at this; there was nothing that could pry Morgan away from him.

Jake held up a hand. "I won't allow that. We have enough leverage with the Feds that I can have my say at the moment. In a strange way it helps us that the FBI has this leak. I don't think the FBI liaison trusts his teams."

He stopped and drank a healthy amount of caffeine and then, placing the coffee back on the table, he sighed.

"Nik, you and Morgan are working on our 'in' with the senator. I agree you are best placed to pull this together but I need your promise that you keep Morgan out of this and in the periphery."

"Of course."

"Beckett obtained some useful information and Manny is currently sifting through it. Work with Manny. We're looking for an in on the senator; some kind of financial information that ties him to his brothers and the family business. Is that okay?" Nik nodded his agreement. "You can't tell me that the senator doesn't have some financial gain from the family itself, so that is the trail we are following. Why was his aide killed by his brothers? Beckett said Elisabeth Costain told him she was close to finding information. What was that information?"

"Manny already sent over some files to the analyst team. I'm going down there after this," Nik confirmed. Manny had a huge area set aside for him and his team on the floor above this one alongside the conference rooms. Analysts, programmers, and Manny the wonder boy himself.

"Adam," Jake began.

Adam switched his attention from what Nik was saying to whatever Jake was giving him to do. Evidently, he wasn't part of Nik's assignment so it was odd they were in the same briefing.

"Even though Alastair is forensically linked to blood on the necklace from the box, there is no body. We couldn't get anything to stick when the party line he is spouting is that it belonged to an ex-girlfriend who liked it rough." Jake shook his head and then worried his lip with his teeth.

Adam watched with growing concern. What the hell was he going to be asked to do?

"We need something on him that will stick and this is where you come in, Adam. Doesn't matter what information we have, unless we can get someone to roll on Alastair we have nothing. Our first port of call is Gareth Headley."

"He's kept it zipped so far." Nik summarized the fact that the cop was staying silent about who paid him to kill Elisabeth, and why, in that single small sentence.

"Dale reported that when he and Joseph Kinnon retrieved Robert Bullen, aka Beckett Jamieson, Greg actually admitted he and Alastair had Elisabeth killed and used Headley as the gunman. It's all hearsay—we don't have a grain in a barn's evidence to go to the DA with."

"Manny couldn't pull anything worthwhile from the files?" Nik asked.

"It isn't officially our job to prove or disprove cases." Jake raised a hand to forestall whatever Nik and Adam were going to say in protestation. "Okay, as much as we get involved, we are here to provide a safe place for people. Although over eighty percent of

Sanctuary operatives are ex-law enforcement, that doesn't mean we can provide a chain of evidence. We're unofficial and unless I give in and get Sanctuary pulled under the Fed umbrella that is the way it stays." He paused briefly. "I need you both out there working on this in full cooperation with the Feds."

Jake wouldn't look him in the eye and Adam frowned. What the hell was going on here? Adam bristled. He couldn't help his instant and visceral reaction. He'd been an FBI agent for five years and look where he'd ended up. Branded dirty and with his freaking heart stomped into a million fragments. The last thing he wanted was to get anywhere close to that agency again.

"We can still work on our own and pass results up the line when we have a chain of evidence situation," Adam said firmly. Jake still wouldn't look him directly in the eye. He was starting to get a very bad feeling about this.

"Liaison won't go for that. They're willing to work with us but only until their own internal leak is plugged. So we need to get this moving. The Feds have a team in place looking into the internal leak." Jake checked his notes. "The Office of Professional Responsibility?" he looked to Adam for confirmation but all Adam could do was nod yes, that is what the department was called. Actually opening his mouth and forming words to vocalize the flood of memories the title bought back was going to be impossible. Freaking FBI internal affairs had destroyed him and his career.

The Office of Professional Responsibly. And Lee Myers.

Jake continued, "Alastair has been released without charge. He says, and I quote, 'it's ridiculous that a woman who is probably alive and partying in the Caribbean is being linked to me as someone I murdered'. Problem is, he's not far off. We don't actually have anything conclusive. Forensics isn't irrefutable and there is apparently other familial DNA on the necklace. We have unsanctioned and limited surveillance in the senator's office that the Alphabets don't know about. But it's been quiet there. Adam, every little thing we have is in the briefing notes I'll give you. Your partner is FBI."

It was no secret Adam was ex-FBI, nor that his time with the security force was cut short when he resigned before charges of bribery or evidence tampering could be thrown at him. No one at Sanctuary ever gave him reason to think they believed he was crooked; hell, Jake wouldn't have hired him if he had thought for one minute Adam was a criminal in Fed clothing.

"Who?"

"You need to stay calm and try and handle this as best you can."

The   words   trickled   into   his

understanding. If Jake was warning him to relax, then there must be some real shit about to rain down on Adam Brooke's world. It couldn't be Lee. Jake wouldn't do that to him. He was the one person who knew about Lee Myers and what he had done. There were hundreds, if not thousands, of FBI operatives out there. And Lee was seconded to internal affairs. They wouldn't send him out to some third-party shit fest.

Everyone knew Adam had left the FBI under a cloud of suspicion. But not everyone knew that the person who had signed the reports indicating Adam's guilt was the very guy who Adam had called best friend and lover. Nik looked confused. Adam didn't blame him—he was probably picking up on the sparks of temper snapping from Adam.

"Who, Jake?" Adam could hear the frustration and heat in his voice.

"You know who it is Adam—"

"No—"

"Look Adam, I don't have a choice, I'm between a rock and a hard place. I've been given an ultimatum. The Feds want in on this case at our level or they take over entirely. It's you working with Lee Myers or we hand Morgan and Beckett over."

Adam stood in a flurry of movement. Playing the Morgan card while Nik was in the room was below the belt but it explained the joint briefing."You heard me. No. I'm not working with the FBI. We don't need them anywhere near this. Not internal affairs. Or Lee freaking Myers." The words snapped from him quickly and with instant heat.

Nik looked confused and Jake's expression hardened from appearing supportive to that of implacability. Clearly this was a point that Jake was going to call as the owner. Seemed like the boss had already agreed things above and beyond Adam's head.

"We have no choice—"

"So get Dale in, or Manny, or hell, Jennifer, Michaela? Anyone else except me to figure him out."

"They asked for you and given I have Feds on my ass every day I'm doing all I can to keep them sweet and happy."

"Fuck Jake, they didn't ask for me. They wouldn't. There's nothing worse to serving FBI than an ex-FBI agent who left covered in crap. If Lee requested this, then there has to be an ulterior motive. What the fuck do they want?" Adam crossed to the window looking down at the city below and the anger and hurt and hate that built inside him was crippling. He never lost his cool like this. But seeing the blond agent back at the bank when he extracted Beckett Jamieson had started to lift the bandage on some very old wounds and Adam was pissed. Why would Lee request to work with him? Adam was everything Lee hated, one of the bad guys, one of the chosen who had fallen.

Instant dislike and his own temper pushed him to remembering. Back there to his last day with Lee handing him papers and surveillance showing Adam compromising his role with the FBI. Back to Lee looking at him like his world had ended. Hell, it wasn't Lee whose world had ended. He heard the door close and glanced up to see Nik had left the room. Well, that was one pressure point gone. Jake moved quietly to stand at his side.

"I wish there was another way, Adam." Jake sounded regretful. "When I started Sanctuary I wanted so badly for this to be a place where we didn't have to deal with all this shit. I hate this as much as you do but when Nik pulled in Morgan it started a chain of falling dominos that I could never have foreseen."

Adam looked at his boss, at the man who had offered him a role at Sanctuary based on Nik's recommendation. Jake had been nothing but fair to him and had trusted him from day one.

"Lee Myers is the lead on this case for the Feds, Adam. He's not with the internal affairs department any more or so I am led to believe. I'm sorry. I don't know what kind of games the Feds in general, or Lee in particular, are playing, but I had no choice in this. I hate it as much as you do."

"I doubt that," Adam snapped. He immediately regretted opening his mouth. He wasn't the loose cannon with no respect for the guy who had given him a safe place to be. He was the stable mass that kept things together, the strong, dependable, and quiet one.

"You're probably right," Jake admitted. "Maybe I don't fully understand any of this Fed crap. At the end of the day I'm just doing what is best for Sanctuary and for the people we protect— people like Morgan and Beckett."

"You don't have to mention them or involve Nik," Adam said wearily. "Bringing Nik into the meeting to make sure I played ball or throwing down the Morgan and Beckett card is unnecessary. You know I would do anything for Sanctuary and I know I owe you—"

Jake's head reared up and he interrupted what Adam was going to say. "You don't owe me shit. From the day Nik told me what had happened to you I knew you were what I wanted for my team. He said he knew you and trusted you. That was good enough for me. You're one of my best operatives and if anything, I owe you. The people you protect owe you. Simply for being the best at what you do and for putting everything to one side to get the job done." Jake placed a hand on his arm and Adam winced at the contact. He couldn't handle emotions as strong as the ones Jake was laying on him. "You do this and we will have your back. The minute you feel like it's all part of some Fed agenda and they are screwing with you, and I mean the absolute minute, you contact Ops and you pull out."

Adam waited a second before answering. Jake giving him an out away from the asshole who had framed him and caused him to leave the FBI was something he didn't need. He was a grown man and he was over the destruction Lee Myers had wrought in his life.

So over it.

CHAPTER 2

Adam scooped up the paperwork and the case codes and left the room. Jake said nothing else to him except a simple "good luck" but Adam was sure he would need a lot more than good luck to deal with Lee Myers.

Apparently his nemesis was waiting the next floor up along with the FBI liaison that was shadowing Jake. In fact, Jake had offered to come up with Adam but he just waved the offer away. If he couldn't handle two FBI agents then he wasn't much of a Sanctuary operative. He pushed through the door to the stairs and climbed the one flight a lot slower than he would normally. At the top of that flight he stopped. The view from this height was magnificent; the city was bathed in post-rain sunlight which sparked off of the glass of tall buildings nearby and created a multitude of prisms. Adam stared blankly out through the window. Somewhere on this floor was the one person who had managed to get under his skin; who had managed to wring from him emotions Adam hadn't even know he had. The same man who listened to lies and believed them and didn't even give Adam the benefit of the doubt, or any trust at all. Hate rose inside Adam. Shit. He thought he had gotten past feeling disappointed by Lee.

Nik caught him as he moved out onto the analyst's floor. Adam's heart twisted at the look on his friend's face.

They had worked together some when both were in the FBI and it had been Adam who hadn't let Nik give up when he was injured. Likewise, as soon as news hit the streets that Adam had been accused of evidence theft, Nik had been there for him. Nik had suggested his name to Jake as a Sanctuary operative and in Adam's mind that meant a lot. Nik hadn't believed any of the accusations that had been thrown at Adam. Still, when enough shit is thrown at you then some of it is likely to stick whoever your friends were. He had lost a lot of good people in his life when his time as an FBI agent came to an end.

"Adam? I'm sorry." Nik sounded worried. It wasn't a good look for the normally uber confident friend he knew.

"It's okay, I said I would do it."

"I know you did," Nik said immediately. "Jeez, I mean, I don't actually know what you decided but I guess I knew you would." Nik ran a hand over his short blond hair and frowned. "I don't know what the fuck the Feds are playing at."

"You and me both," Adam replied. All he knew was that he felt as if he was being blackmailed and it was hard to keep his temper in check.

"Thank you," Nik held up a hand when Adam opened his mouth to interrupt, "I mean it.

I know this is nothing less than blackmail and for keeping Morgan with us. Thank you."

They shook hands and Nik pulled him close for a moment. It was enough for Adam to draw on Nik's energy and to keep going when all he wanted to do was hit something.

He didn't wait to compose himself. He could be professional and just get on with the damn job. Pushing open the door to the small conference room he startled both people inside. It was petty but hell, petty worked for him today.

Ignoring the tall dark-haired guy at the window as not important his gaze zeroed in on the man now standing by the table in the middle. Lee's face held an expression of intense focus and he took a step toward Adam. For a brief second Adam felt the incomparable urge to go to the man he had called friend and lover and kiss him. Of course that lasted for a very split second. It was soon pushed aside by anger.

Adam swallowed the desire to get Lee to go that sat on the tip of his tongue. He was a professional and he had a job to do.

"Myers," Adam said formally.

The liaison shadow came closer from the window to stand next to Lee. He extended his hand.

" Sean Hanson," the shadow said carefully, ", FBI liaison to Sanctuary."

Adam shook his hand but he didn't take his eyes off of Lee. There were no wasted words. This Sean Hanson guy didn't introduce Lee to Adam and he certainly didn't enquire if they knew each other. Adam's file was clear for any agent to see, as well as his assignment history with Lee. No one knew about their other off-the-records relationship. Not unless Lee had decided that fell under a need to know banner and this liaison was on the list of those who needed to know.

The silence was nearing awkward but

Adam was damned if he was going to start the ball rolling. He was still struggling with his temper and it didn't matter how calm he appeared on the outside, he was far from it on the inside.

"It's good to see you, Adam," Lee finally offered in his carefully modulated tones. His preppy background showed in every inch of him from his tailored dark gray suit to the shine on his three hundred dollar shoes, and from the crisp white shirt to the burgundy tie knotted just so. The way he looked was what had attracted Adam to him in the first place. Call him shallow but Lee was stereotypical upper class and Adam always enjoyed the role of being the bit of rough on the side.

Five inches shorter than him, and thirty pounds lighter, Lee was the complete opposite to his own six-three wide frame. Lee was blond, Adam brunet, Lee's eyes sparked silver-blue, his own were brown. Nothing could mark them as different as much as their physical appearances. That didn't even begin to scratch the surface of what lay beneath the window dressing. Adam was volatile, impulsive, Lee thought and considered and weighed up pros and cons. This was infuriating, tedious, and at the same time so damn alluring.

Long eyelashes framed those eerily clear silver-blue eyes and his hair was shorter than Adam remembered. Shorter than when they had met in the vault during the Beckett retrieval. Fuck. Two minutes and he was just about to open his mouth and comment on an ex-lovers hair. For fuck's sake!

"How is your operative? The one who was shot?" Lee placed a hand on his own chest as he asked.

"He's fine." There. Short answer to a stupidly lame question.

"And you made it away with Beckett." Lee frowned briefly as he said this. It was quick but Adam caught it before it disappeared. Evidently it still rankled with Lee that Sanctuary had won that particular face-off over who took the witness.

"Yes."

Lee narrowed his gaze at the short answer. "I'll need more than that."

"Beckett is in our care. The FBI has had their time to debrief."

Lee crossed his arms over his chest. "You do realize this is a cross-agency operation now. The FBI and Sanctuary need to work together on this."

"If you say so," Adam replied offhand.

"I'll leave you two to hash things out," Sean interrupted. "If you would excuse me." Sean inclined his head and left the room with no other words. Lee and Adam faced off like two combatants in an arena.

As soon as the door shut Lee was on him with what he really wanted to say. He took a step closer until they were nearly toe to toe. "I don't give a shit about being polite. You're reporting to me in this case, Brooke."

"Like hell I am," Adam snapped vehemently.

Lee, damn him, simply raised an eyebrow in a mocking gesture. "This is a Federal case against organized crime. You may have Beckett but this isn't kids playing, this is FBI jurisdiction—"

"Always the big picture with you." Adam poked a finger into Lee's chest. "Never the cogs—"

"What the fuck do you mean by that?" Lee grabbed his finger and pushed it away. His gaze narrowed.

"Beckett would have been what to you?" Adam clenched his fists at his side. "Just a means to an end? Someone you could put in crosshairs to get to the senator and Alastair?"

"Where the hell is that coming from—"

"I'm working with you because I have to Lee. *With you.* Not for you. Not for the FBI. This may well be interagency, but remember Sanctuary isn't part of your freaking alphabet soup."

"You need us. Sanctuary doesn't know shit about how to handle a case like this," Lee retorted. He took another step closer. They were nearly nose to nose and emotions were high.

"Like the Feds have any idea what a case looks like," Adam said heatedly. "They're as corrupt as the people they claim to investigate."

"Just because they threw you out—"

"I freaking resigned."

"Same difference." Lee dismissed Adam's words with anger in his tone. Then he appeared to consciously pull himself together. "Look, Adam." Lee touched a hand to Adam's arm. "Can we not start all this shit again? This is stupid."

"Don't touch me." Adam took a step

back and Lee pulled his hand away like he had been burned.

"Look, I'm willing to let the past lie. I don't know why you did it. If it was for money, or you were forced too—"

"What?" Adam couldn't believe Lee was bringing this up.

"I'm sure you thought you were doing the right thing." Lee's voice was firm but it verged on earnest and forgiving. "I'm willing to forget and forgive for the sake of the case."

"You're going to do what?" Adam heard the warning in his own voice and a flicker of apprehension passed over Lee's face. He drew himself to his full height.

"Adam. We need to move past this if we want to have any chance of dealing with the case."

Despite his chest being tight and red flooding his mind Adam started calmly enough. "Move past this? How the hell do we move past this? My partner, nearly from day one as a Fed, the man who had my back, the one who I respected and trusted, jeez, the man I thought I was in love with, saw some shit piece of evidence. All of a sudden I am a criminal? You never even asked for my side."

"There aren't sides to be seen," Lee said patiently. "You did what you did. The end." Lee's silver-blue eyes held no real expression. Suddenly he was stony faced and completely in control. The ice man to Adam's heat.

"I. Didn't. Do. What they said—"

"I saw the photos."

"You saw photos? Fuck, Lee. Did you never think of believing me over them?" Voices were raised and heated. Any minute now someone was going to come back in the room and ask them what the fuck was going on.

"No." Plainly Lee didn't have to think about that. "I had those photos tested. I wanted to believe you so bad. Believe that you wouldn't betray the Bureau—"

"The Bureau? Don't you mean you—"

Lee ignored him and ploughed on. "You know what I found, Adam? Huh?"

Adam knew all too well what the results would be. Photos of him receiving a package from a lawyer in an on-going trial. And every single one would be legitimate.

Lee continued, "They hadn't been tampered with. Not a single one was photoshopped. I know what I saw."

"You didn't look hard enough—" Adam shouted. He hadn't expected anyone to look deeper than the surface. No one except Lee.

Lee didn't let him talk. "I'm willing to forget them. And fuck," Lee ran a hand over his hair in a gesture of frustration. "I thought I loved you too and you destroyed that—"

Adam couldn't stop himself. His regrets and his temper were high and clashing wildly in his head. All he could focus on was the man who stood in front of him who didn't believe in Adam. Who hadn't supported him or stopped to consider anything outside of those black and white photos. Lee talked about Adam destroying him? Hell, Adam had been just as shattered by Lee instantly believing his lover capable of deceit.

He shoved Lee. Every single cell in his body wanted to pummel him into the ground and work off some of the anger. Lee pushed back with a barely contained snarl. That was it. The final nail. With hard shoves and barely thought out curses, he forced Lee back and back until the man's thighs reached the table. Lee had him pegged as a man with nothing, but Adam could prove he still had something in the only way he could ever best his lover. Temper was turning into lust. He never could get enough of Lee and missed the lithe body beneath his. In seconds Adam had Lee twisted facedown on the wood with one hand grabbing both of his and holding him, and the other pulling at his belt.

Lee struggled briefly with colorful curses leaving his mouth and then, just as suddenly he wasn't fighting. If anything he was lifting his ass so Adam could pull off his pants and finally Adam had his hand around Lee's dick, his own hard as a rock and pushed insistently into the crease of Lee's ass. Adam was rutting and pulling and twisting Lee's dick as he forced the smaller guy to ride the table. Lee turned his head and Adam leaned down just that bit farther to kiss and bite and demand more by touch alone.

It was just as he remembered. The scent of Lee. The taste of him needy and wanting. The noises his lover made when he was being fucked. All that stopped Adam from having skin-to-skin contact were the layers of material; without them he could be inside. The thought of being buried deep in Lee was nearly enough to push him over the edge.

"Please," Lee moaned from beneath him. The word snapped through the desire to take and Adam instantly let go. He stumbled backward blindly until his back hit the wall and he slumped over with his hands on his knees and his breathing harsh and rapid. What the fuck had just happened? What the hell was he playing at? He hated the man, he didn't want to fuck him.

Lee lay across the table for a few seconds, probably gathering his thoughts and then he stood upright. All the while avoiding Adam's gaze he tucked his shirt in and pulled his pants closer before buttoning and tightening his belt. Straightening his tie and running a hand through his hair he quickly became Lee FBI, not the Lee who was debauched, calling for more, and who nearly got fucked over a table in the conference room. With an unlocked door. Adam groaned and dropped his head in defeat. An unlocked door for God's sake.

"Adam?" Lee sounded lost but when

Adam finally looked at the man who was casually leaning back against the table he could swear there was pity on his face. Or something akin to it. Pity? Or maybe empathy? Adam couldn't tell and he needed neither. Very deliberately Lee reached down and arranged his crotch. The outline of his dick was still visible but Adam had lost his erection as soon as the terrible mistake they were making hit him upside the head. "It's still there for us," Lee added almost sadly.

"I never said we didn't fuck well. Looking back it was about the only thing we did have," Adam finally said. Reaching into his pocket he pulled out his keys. "We're leaving and I'm driving."

Lee indicated piles of files. "Hang on. We haven't looked at these, or created a strategy. We don't even know where we're going—"

Adam wasn't willing to stay in this room

a moment longer. And one guaranteed way to screw with Lee's head was to throw chaos into any suggested careful planning. "Bring the files. We'll decide in the car."

CHAPTER 3

"Get in," Adam bit out.

Lee didn't hesitate. Adam was in just the sort of frame of mind to drive off and leave him standing in the parking lot like an idiot. Placing the files on the dash he put on his belt and then pulled them down onto his lap. He tried to focus on the contents of the papers. Images, stories, and notes from cases spreading back to the 1980s but all he could see in his head was what had just happened. Pushed flat on the table and with Adam heavy against him after so long it was a surprise he hadn't lost it there and then. Christ, he'd missed Adam. All the stages of grief he had worked through after losing him meant nothing when he was in the same freaking space as him breathing the same air.

Tall and broad with dark brown eyes and dark hair the man was gorgeous. Lee knew there was a soft furring of hair on his broad chest and that same hair started just again below his navel. He remembered the weight of Adam's dick, the length of it, the shape of it. If Lee closed his eyes he could picture every second they were ever together. Assigned to the mopping up of a murder case as newbie partners they had clicked immediately. Whatever they said about opposites attracting was true. Not only physically were they diametrically opposed, but also in the way they worked. Adam led with his heart. He always had. He was the heroic idiot who stood in the way of bullets and fists alike, who protected Lee with both his body and his quick reactions. Lee was the thinker, the planner, the one who wanted to wait and analyze. They had made such a damn good team. One that cleared cases and made their rise in the FBI quick and painless. They worked and lived for their country and when back at Adam's apartment after a fateful shootout where Lee had been pinned down by a drug dealer and Adam had thrown himself at the guy, they had made love.

Never sex. It had never been sex. Not for Lee. Hell, Lee had fallen in love with the big guy about a day after meeting him. They bickered like an old married couple but they got the job done and finally everything made sense in Lee's world. Every memory of ex-boyfriends was wiped clean, every heartbreak healed. He was in love and content with his place in life and the person he was with.

When the chance for Lee came to move to the department dealing with the internal affairs of the FBI he jumped at it. He didn't see it as jumping ship on Adam. Adam was training new guys and doing it damned well. Their FBI partnership had run its course and some separation made Lee fall more in love every day. Lee's analytical brain made him perfect for the kinds of analysis he had to carry out and every day, if Adam wasn't on a case, he went home to the man he loved.

What could be better than that?

If Adam became that bit more taciturn or remote, if his explanations of what had happened in his work became less detailed and more sketchy, Lee didn't think to question. Lee's own work by necessity was kept under wraps. Investigations inside the FBI were difficult at best.

"Where do we start, Brains?"

Lee was jolted from his thoughts by the use of his old nickname. He looked across to Adam who was staring at him with expectation on his face.

"It's been a while since I was in field work," he apologized. Then he mentally hit himself upside the head. Why the hell did he say that? "Uhm." He opened file one. "I looked at the parties to the case. If we can't get to Alastair direct then we need to do a Capone and get him on something indirect."

"I should imagine he has his taxes up to date," Adam interrupted sarcastically.

Lee ignored him. "I'm thinking laterally here. We should be looking at the people working for him. The cop who killed the girl. He's not talking about who had him shoot her, or why. But if we go after that side we could get a handle on what makes Alastair tick."

"Agreed."

"Why was the girl killed? She was the senator's aide so why did she need to die? What did she know? What did the Bullens have on the cop to make him do their dirty work? Why a cop? Why not a random street kid? And the information shows the cop's family was pulled into this." He stopped and flicked through papers until he found what he wanted. "A wife and son, both refused witness protection they were offered. Margaret 'Maggie' Headley, and Joshua, her only child, is aged twenty-four. Joshua is some kind of genius studying criminology for a doctorate. Probably took a lot of money for education like that."

"It's a start."

"Reports say the wife and son didn't give authorities much. Denied knowing anything, don't visit Gareth Headley in jail. Basically they've cut him out of their lives for all intents and purposes. They weren't investigated further. Totally squeaky clean."

"Everyone has skeletons in their closets. Rule one—always start with the family."

CHAPTER 4

The address they had for Maggie Headley led them to a building of apartments stacked one on top of the other and eight to a floor for at least ten floors. The elevator was broken and they completed the climb to floor six in absolute silence. The graffiti on the first few floors carried gang colors and both men had their guns under their jackets. It wasn't the best place to live and Lee thought it was a far cry from the detached post war house the Headleys had lived in before all this went down. Of course it was likely the original house had been paid for out of pay-offs so it was a place built on sand.

They knocked on the door of apartment six B and waited. Adam had muscled his way to the front. Seemed like old habits died hard. The door opened on a chain and a woman's face peered out through the small space. Her eyes widened at the two men and Lee didn't blame her. Adam never had learned to tone down his fierce expression.

"Ma'am," Lee passed her his credentials but didn't announce who he was. Last thing the woman needed was for an FBI agent to announce his presence in a place reeking of drugs and littered with gang graffiti. She took the wallet and shut the door on him. There was a phone number for her to call. Lee imagined that was what she was doing to verify who he was.

"She's taking her time," Adam muttered irritably. "We should probably push the door in." He flexed his not inconsiderable muscles and Lee placed a gentling hand on his arm. Adam used to react to that touch with a rueful smile but all Lee got now was a flash of temper in his ex-lover's gorgeous eyes.

"Cool it, big guy," Lee muttered in return. Adam looked like he wanted to say something but the door opened at that moment and a thin, pale, and rather nervous looking woman asked them inside.

As soon as the door shut she moved into the tiny kitchenette which separated living space and cooking area. Only once she had the counter between her and the two men did she perceivably relax.

"I called my son, he had gone to the store," she said quickly.

Lee nodded. Calling the son would make sense. "I won't say anything until he gets here." They stood uneasily looking at each other for a moment. The silence was unnerving. He hated silences. No one ever learned anything by being silent.

"You have a nice apartment here, Mrs Headley," Lee lied. And then he wished he hadn't opened his mouth at all.

Jeez, she looked like she was going to cry. "Here? On the sixth floor of a building that needs condemning? How can you even say that?"

"I'm sorry—"

"I had a beautiful house. Double fronted. And a yard. Our neighbors looked out for us and we were happy. This." She gestured wildly around her. The move seemed out of character for such a small woman. "This is nothing but a punishment for us."

Silence again.

"How long will your son be, Mrs Headley?" Adam pointedly looked at his watch. Lee could feel his partner's tension from where he stood. This was not a good sign.

"Not long," she answered quickly. Lee watched as she clenched and unclenched her hands then placed them flat on the counter surface. "Could I get you a coffee or a cold drink?" she asked.

"Water," Adam said.

"Coffee. Cream. One sugar," Lee answered. Adam shot him a look. That look that spoke so much and was telling him they weren't staying long enough to drink freaking coffee. Lee raised an eyebrow in response. Maggie Headley quickly donned the façade of hostess and placed water and a coffee on the counter along with a small and very delicate plate of cookies. The offering was so much out of what should be in this small place. It was civility and normality and he could see her relax inch by inch. He sat next to Adam on a small sofa and halfway through his coffee and three small cookies they were interrupted as the door flew open and a wild-eyed young man came into the apartment. He was out of breath and his whole body screamed offense.

Adam immediately stood and pulled himself to his full height, Lee was slower to rise.

"Mom?" Josh Headley moved quickly to his mom's side and grasped her arm. "Are you okay?"

"They're FBI, Joshy."

At this he rounded on Lee and Adam. "What the hell do you want?"

"Just to ask a few questions," Lee began.

"No. No more questions. We have nothing else to say to you."

"You knew what your father was involved in, didn't you?" Adam asked accusingly.

Lee shot him a quick look. Adam was clearly not running by the rulebook.

"We didn't know anything," Maggie said. Her hand rested on her throat and her face was devoid of color.

"Well that's bullshit," Adam snapped.

Josh took the few steps to face off with Adam. Shorter and lighter, he was still standing up to Adam, as if will alone was going to drop the larger man to the floor. Lee had to admire the bravery of the guy.

"Fuck you," Josh had anger dripping

from his voice. "Take your badges and your guns and leave us alone. We've told you everything we know."

"You've told us nothing," Adam near bellowed.

Give him his due, Josh didn't back down. Lee hesitated to step in. He didn't know what Adam was playing at but for a few more seconds he would let this play. Maybe there was a game plan?

Josh clenched his hands into fists, much as his mom did earlier, and gave Lee the impression he might come out swinging. There was an awful lot of anger inside Josh. Even a casual observer could see that.

"What do you want to hear? The lies he told us? About the money deposited into bank accounts for what he had done that we gave to charity? You already know all that."

Lee thought back to the files in the car. There wasn't really anything else they had said.

"We don't know anything else."

"Why?" Lee said softly. He moved subtly in between Adam and Josh who both took a step back and away from him. Josh in surprise, Adam probably in disgust at being stopped.

"Why what?" Maggie replied.

"Why did he do it? Did you have debt? Was he gambling? Were there medical bills to pay?"

"No. Nothing like that. I already said all this." Maggie looked at her son with wide eyes and a pleading expression. "I don't know why he did that awful thing—"

"This is harassment," Josh snapped.

His interruption stopped his mom in full flow and her hand fluttered from her throat to her mouth. She caught Lee's gaze and looked away. You didn't have to be able to read people to know she was withholding something.

Josh took a step closer to his mom. "My boyfriend is a lawyer," he said. "You can't do this to us—"

"Your mom asked us in," Lee explained evenly. He wasn't going to comment on the lawyer remark. A lawyer wasn't going to stop Lee and Adam getting to the bottom of this. Anyway after seeing Maggie's reaction there was no way he was leaving without seeing what she was keeping back.

"What are you studying?" Lee changed the subject.

"What?"

"At NYU? It's a doctorate, is that right?"

"PhD in criminology." Josh looked at him suspiciously.

"Guess education like that isn't cheap," Lee said conversationally.

"I work," Josh snapped. "You think my dad killed a girl and destroyed years of good policing for me to get my degrees? My grandparents left me money."

Adam moved in a heartbeat and in a

repeat of what he had done to Lee this morning he had Josh facedown on the counter. Only this time it wasn't sexual. Fuck. Was he reading Josh his rights? Adam wasn't a freaking cop.

"…anything you say will be used against you in court…"

"Leave my son alone. He's not done anything—" Maggie was clawing at Adam's arm.

"Let me up," Josh was shouting.

Lee moved as his brain caught up with what was happening.

"…attorney will be provided at no cost…" Adam's voice was calm in amongst the chaos.

"Adam—" Lee pulled at his other arm but Adam wasn't moving. He was gripping Josh and reading him his freaking rights like he had all the power to do so. "We're arresting you for withholding information pertinent—"

"Wait. Wait!" Maggie was nearly

hysterical. She had taken a step back from Adam and her son. "There's a list. Stop. I'll get it. Please stop."

Adam released Josh from his position over the counter but still gripped an arm. He stared down at Maggie with an implacable gaze on his face. All Lee could think was what the hell was going on? He caught Adam's gaze and there was nothing there. No hint of what the fuck the other man was playing at. Maggie backed away, tears falling down her cheeks. Then she took a box marked Christmas from a tall shelf in the corner of the apartment. Rummaging inside she pulled out a bundle of Christmas cards tied with a red ribbon. She held it close to her chest.

"It's all that is keeping us alive—" she said brokenly.

"Mom?" Josh pulled away from Adam's grip and Lee was relieved when Adam let him go. In two strides he had his mom in a hug.

"What is it?"

"He said I should keep them. That if I had them then they wouldn't touch us." She raised a trembling hand to Josh's face. "Touch you."

"Who said, Mom?"

"Your father."

Josh guided her to sit on the sofa. "What are they?"

Shakily she held the pile out to Lee who took it carefully from her. After pulling the ribbon the cards were loose in his hands but inside, buried deep in amongst velvet and poetry, was a small notebook no bigger than a few inches across.

"Once," she said. "He did wrong once. That's all. We've been paying for it ever since."

Lee flicked through the book. A list of names, dates, observations, all in the same sloping scrawl of one person. A couple of names jumped out and he guessed the analysts back at the office could pull something out of the meaningless jumble of codes and symbols.

"Gareth said if I let it out of my sight then they would know and it would be the end of things for him and us. He told them... told them that there was evidence stacked away at a bank, somewhere. Copies of this notebook. They never looked to me. They asked him to kill the girl and he said no. They told him if he didn't they were going to kill Josh. That it didn't matter what he had to use against them. I'm so sorry."

"It's fine, Mom." Josh was holding her close. He may well be reassuring his mom but he didn't look so calm himself.

"They weren't going to kill our sweet boy, your dad wouldn't let them," she said between sobs. "He was so sorry. *Always so sorry.* But we couldn't let them hurt you."

Adam had moved to one side and was on his cell. Lee shook his head. This wasn't how he'd expected this to go down.

"We need to take this information. You understand this could be exactly what we need to connect the dots with Alastair and finally get charges to stick. If he's put away then you'd be safe." Lee was lying. Even he could hear it in his voice.

"It could also be nothing." Josh was resigned and he shook his head. "It may be a freaking laundry list, it doesn't have to be evidence or any kind of naming names."

"I'm sure they watch us," Maggie interrupted. Fear haunted her eyes. "It's a balance you see. They leave us alone and Gareth stays quiet. But if that balance tips—"

"We'll get you to a safe house," Adam announced as he ended the call.

"We're not going anywhere," Josh said defiantly.

"Call it a holiday." Adam wasn't listening. Instead he was crossing to the window to look out onto the street below.

"You can't make us leave," Josh protested. "I have a life, my degree—"

"Josh." Maggie's voice was thick with tears. "I don't want to be here anymore."

Josh stared at his mom. Confusion and worry was etched into his expression and he turned to look at a bookcase with a single sad pile of magazines on the third shelf from the top, offering everyone else his back. He slumped, defeat showing in every line of his body. Lee waited for him to turn and quickly agree to leave. Instead, straightening of his spine, he turned back to face Lee with determination on his face.

"Take my mom," he said firmly. "Make sure she's safe. I'm not going with you." His own startlingly green eyes, just like his mom's, were suspiciously bright with unshed tears. Whether because of grief or anger Lee couldn't tell.

"Don't be so damn stupid," Adam snapped.

Lee stopped his partner from talking with a raised hand. "We can't make you go," he said. "But I want to keep you safe."

Adam backed down from his confrontational stance and Lee considered what he should say. In the end he said nothing as Maggie did all the persuading for him.

"I'm scared, Josh. Please don't leave me on my own."

The expressions passing over Josh's face ranged from angry to despairing to accepting. Finally Josh sat quietly. Then, visibly making a decision, he rose to his feet and pulled his mom with him.

"Let's pack a few of your things," he said softly. They disappeared through the only other door. Lee took a moment to calm down and looked about him at the evidence of life in this small place. He assumed that through the only other door was the mother's room. The sofa in this main room was set up as a bed with a cascade of blankets and there was a Grisham and two books with unpronounceable titles lying on the floor next to an empty glass. He supposed that was where Josh had been sleeping. If the duffle on the floor was any indication then the young guy was living out of a single bag. He glimpsed inside the second room when the door opened. It didn't look much better in there than it did out here. He waited patiently—he had a lot to say and he needed mother and son out of the room so he could speak his mind openly.

As soon as the door shut behind mother and son he rounded on Adam.

"What the hell was that?" he whispered loudly but didn't stop to listen to a reply. "Warn me next time you want to throw the rules out of the window and play good cop bad cop." Lee was holding tight to his anger now that the immediate issue had passed.

"You saw she was hiding something," Adam said drily and just as low in volume. "I used the skills I have—"

Lee couldn't stop the incredulousness in his voice. "Beating and threatening a kid—"

Adam huffed a quiet laugh. "I didn't beat on him—"

"You threatened him though."

"Not like I was going to carry through on an arrest. I'm not a cop."

Like that made any sense at all. Pretending to be a cop made it all okay? "What happened to procedure? There are more subtle ways—" Lee pushed his fingers through his short hair and then left his hand there for a moment, twisted in it. The sharp twinge of pain grounded him for a second. It didn't last long when Adam huffed a laugh.

"Screw subtle," he bit out harshly. "You and your pansy-ass FBI rules weren't going to push her. Only thinking her son was in trouble was going to do that. You see a weakness, you go for it."

"What the hell? Weakness? These are people. You're not some renegade and you're not outside the law." Lee was right up in Adam's face.

"Never said I was." Adam looked down and nonchalantly examined his fingers. Like nothing mattered. Like threatening the son was the right thing to do. Christ. This man knew how to press every single one of Lee's irritation and temper buttons. "Her weakness is her son. We got what we wanted. Job done."

"Job done. What's wrong with you?"

"Wrong with me?" Adam looked confused. Shit. Did Adam really think he had done nothing wide of the mark? "There's nothing wrong with me."

"It never used to be just about you getting the job done." Lee sounded horrified. Adam was impetuous and quick thinking but forcing a desperate woman's hand by threatening to arrest her son? That was way past acceptable.

Adam looked up and his expression changed from calm to hell on earth in a split second. "Don't question what I do or how I do it," he spat out. "You no longer have the right."

Lee ignored this. He was on his soapbox and still very firmly in horrified mode. "No wonder the FBI is worried about Sanctuary if this is what it's about. What are you? A band of rebels that think they're above the law?" Lee hated and regretted the words as soon as they left his mouth. Rebels? Why did he use that word? "I'm sorry—"

Adam's lips thinned and he leaned close. "You wanna know why I cut the corners there? Huh?" Adam plowed on, "I want this finished 'cause the sooner it's ended the faster you can fuck off out of my life."

They had retreated to opposite corners when Josh and his mom came back out of her room. Maggie had packed two small carry-ons and Josh scooped his own duffle, a phone charger and the two books. He left the Grisham. In those bags was their life and for a few seconds Lee felt a heavy weight of guilt that they were doing this.

Part of him felt Maggie and Josh should go to a FBI safe house; but it wasn't a big part. He didn't even begin to argue with Adam over this. There was still the unplugged leak. The same leak connected to Morgan Drake, the Bullens and God knows what else. Whatever his opinion of Sanctuary after what he had just seen Adam do, he wasn't going to compromise the woman who, in fear of her life, had protected her husband's secrets for so long.

"I need to phone Eric, my boyfriend." Josh was firm and gripped his cell tightly.

"No phone calls, not to family, not to

friends. Not even to the boyfriend," Adam said dispassionately. Lee frowned. Adam sounded hard, implacable, and it wasn't the Adam whom Lee had loved. In fact, Lee had to face the fact there was nothing of the Adam that Lee had loved in the man who stood before him, not one speck.

Adam took the cell from Josh's hands and turned it over. Removing the SIM he dropped it to the floor and smashed it with the heel of his boot. Josh said nothing; he looked shocked at first but then merely resigned.

"Phone stays here," Adam said. He threw it on top of the blankets on the sofa. "Do you have a cell, Ma'am?"

Maggie blinked at him in confusion. Lee was worried she was close to losing it.

"No," she said. "I don't have a phone. Is that important? I don't understand." She looked to Josh who simply pulled her in for a close hug.

"Mom has never had a phone," he

explained. "What will happen to my dad? Have you thought about that?"

Adam looked at Lee to answer this and Lee wasn't sure where to start. "I'll pass this on to Sanctuary. They can talk to prison services or the Feds," he reassured. "We will ensure that he's in a secure wing."

"Thank you," Maggie said a little breathlessly.

"You okay, Mom?" Josh was worried.

She leaned against him. "I will be," she said simply.

CHAPTER 5

"Why didn't you take the chance of witness protection?" Lee asked of both mom and son when they had been in the car for ten minutes and were now heading out of the city and north.

"We weren't interested," Josh said simply. His mom made a small noise of agreement.

Lee winced inwardly. There were a lot of reasons why someone wouldn't want to get tangled in with the FBI. He was well-versed in dealing with cases where people felt the FBI couldn't protect them. With internal problems God knew how safe anyone was. But saying they didn't need protection made them nothing more than naive.

Lee chanced a look at Adam. His partner was focused entirely on the road, his expression stony. Adam knew as well as Lee that Gareth

Headley would surely have been offered some kind of arrangement for his family.

Josh continued. "The deal my dad made was much higher than you. It was with Alastair Bullen himself. Nothing the cops offered was going to better us *all* staying alive."

Lee recalled the information he had on the cop. There had been two serious attempts on his life inside and more than one incidence of intimidation and low-level violence. It didn't seem to help that Headley was in a safe wing away from the general populace. Somehow people got through to hurt him. That could have been just because he was a cop. A cop in jail was open season for any and all matters of revenge. The two serious attempts on Headley's life had been made to look random but no one was fooled. One way or another it appeared the Bullen family wanted the cop gone.

"So your dad leaves your mom with enough to keep her, and you, safe," Lee summarized. "Didn't you ever think he would do something like that?"

Maggie spoke this time. "There's a copy of the whole thing with lawyers, to be released in the event of his death, or ours. Josh didn't know about it."

"You deliberately withheld evidence—"

"Tell me you wouldn't have done the same thing as my mom." Josh wasn't arguing. "If that damn book is all there is between us and a bullet what else could she do?" He sounded tired. Lee didn't answer and everyone sat in silence as the car ate the miles.

After an hour Adam checked in with Sanctuary. He exchanged codes and instructions but the only thing in the whole jumbled mess that Lee recognized was his name and the names of the Headley family. The codes they used were very different from the FBIs.

"Where are we heading?" He finally couldn't contain his curiosity. Adam flashed a brief look at him but didn't immediately answer. Lee ignored the deliberate snub and turned to look out of the window. Following the natural progression of direction on I87 they were heading north and away from Albany. They passed signs for Pharaoh Lake and then stopped near there for a break and fuel. By unspoken agreement Lee stayed with Josh when he used the bathroom and Adam waited outside of the ladies for Maggie. Josh was skirting Adam when they got anywhere near each other. Lee didn't blame the guy. Adam was a hulking, brooding presence who didn't spare a smile for anyone.

Bundled back into the car it was Lee's role to pay and grab drinks. Then within ten minutes of stopping they were back on the road. The signs Lee noticed leading to Westport East and Elizabethtown had him questioning just how far north they were damn well going.

"Adam?" he finally gave in and asked

again. These safe houses may be need to know but jeez, this was a joint operation.

"Eight. We're taking them to eight." Adam's voice was low and Lee imagined the two in the back seat wouldn't be able to hear.

"Where is eight?"

"You'll see when you get there."

"For fuck's sake," Lee snapped. His voice was louder and Adam followed suit.

"Sharing shit with *your* FBI is off my 'to do' list." He emphasized the 'your' and Lee could have bet money that not only would the passengers hear the words but also pick up on the intonation. It took less than a few seconds and Josh leaped in to the conversation.

"Wait." Josh's voice held a note of worry that was verging on hysteria. Lee groaned inwardly. Hell, they hadn't covered the whole not really entirely an FBI operation problem. "Stop the car."

If anything Adam sped up. Lee glanced

in the vanity mirror; Maggie was clinging tightly to Josh who in turn looked overwhelmed and scared. He turned in his seat.

"Did you lie to us?" Josh asked. Lee wondered for a moment what Josh expected him to say. If indeed Lee was one of the bad guys then lying would probably be his whole motivation.

"Trust us, I'm FBI. Adam isn't."

"He's a cop, right?" Josh said quickly. Lee thought back to Adam pinning Josh to the kitchen surface and reading him his rights.

"Yeah," he lied. It was easier. He glanced at the odometer. One hundred fifty miles already and the landscape was changing. Instead of views of hills and trees the fringe of actual forest was getting closer. When Adam's cell sounded he took one look at the screen and pulled over on the side of the road. Stopping the engine he pulled the keys from the ignition and left the 4x4 with a terse "Stay here".

Lee repeated the same words to a confused Josh and Maggie and clambered out of the car as quickly as he could. In a few long strides he caught up with Adam who was speaking rapidly into the phone.

"Adam—"

Adam held up a hand to hush him and continued his conversation.

"I can leave him here," he said. He was staring right at Lee, with a frighteningly blank expression on his face. "I'm not sure we can trust him with the location."

What the hell?

Adam continued, "He's FBI. They don't have a handle on the leak, let alone us."

"Give me the phone," Lee demanded. Adam simply stood taller and half turned away from Lee showing him his broad back.

"He's here," Adam said. Quirking a sardonic smile in Lee's direction he added, "He's pissed. I'm not kidding around here; I have two people in my care—"

"Our care"

"—and I'm not happy with him being here."

Lee could have punched the guy to the floor at that very moment. It wasn't him that had broken the law and betrayed the team, was it? No, it was Adam that had decided to walk the fine line between right and wrong. Hell, Lee had the photos to prove it.

"Give me the phone," he repeated.

"I want it on record that I don't agree," Adam was saying. He nodded and then with a final "okay" he ended the call and made to walk back to the car. Lee stopped him with a firm hand on Adam's arm. Adam shrugged off the hand.

"Get in the car, Lee." Clearly the order was totally against what Adam felt.

"I'm not the bad guy here," Lee said firmly.

"And you're saying I am?" Adam snapped.

Lee let out the sigh that had built inside him. He didn't mean that and Adam knew it. "For God's sake, Adam—"

Adam leaned down and gripped Lee's arm to the point of pain. Lee refused to let the man know it hurt. He was focusing intently on the sparking temper in Adam's eyes. "I'm telling you this once, Myers, and I won't say it again. You're a Fed. I don't trust Feds, I don't trust you, and I would rather drop the Headleys back at the Air Force base we just passed than bring whoever is fucking around in the FBI to the doorstep of one of our safe houses." He released Lee's arm to walk back to the 4x4 and to Josh who was standing outside the car looking uncertain and fearful.

"What have I done to make you not trust *me*?" Lee asked loudly.

Adam stopped, turned and took the few

steps back to Lee. "You're blind. You don't see things right in front of your eyes. I don't trust you, because when I look at you, I don't know you." Adam didn't give Lee a chance to reply and in a short time he sat back in the car.

The engine started and Adam checked Josh was in the rear seat. Lee inhaled of the fresh cool air. That had stung. Stung a lot. They used to know each other so well. Like brothers, then when they'd become lovers they worked together so seamlessly. Right up until the last case. Grief bit sharp inside him. At the loss of a friend, and a lover.

"It's no more than half an hour from here," Adam announced as Lee was buckling his belt. Lee concentrated on the scenery as they passed and wondered what they would find when they hit this Sanctuary eight.

Sanctuary was on the FBI radar for many reasons. Yes, they did good work in the main, helping people out that couldn't get the assistance from normal sources. But, with no regulations, or rules, or hell, anything in the way of accountability, it was just a bunch of renegade idiots playing with the law. No wonder Sean had asked him to shadow this case.

CHAPTER 6

The place itself was nothing awe inspiring and Adam hadn't been to this particular safe house before. Clearly built as a summer house some time back, the edges of the house blurred into the forest and the small area in front of it had been cleared for parking the 4x4. Adam was out with gun drawn as soon as the vehicle stopped and much to his irritation Lee followed suit. Together they checked the perimeter and Adam noted the few paths up and away from the back of the place. As usual there would be some kind of way out of the house if they needed to run.

"How is it the military doesn't know about this place?" Lee mused out loud. "Given the local air force base then surely the set-up has been spotted at some point."

Adam pushed his irritation with Lee to one side and didn't answer. Perimeter secure and with Ops telling him in his ear that everything was quiet it was time to move everyone inside.

Back at the car Maggie was leaning against her son and she looked very pale. Her countenance worried Adam. This retrieval had been on the fly and so damned fast he had nothing on any medical history. She looked old enough, maybe late fifties, to suffer from all manner of ailments that Adam wasn't qualified to handle. Every safe house had medical supplies but what if what she needed wasn't here? First things first, he needed intel on this situation. Then he had to bed down and get his head around this change in his day. From interviewing for a lead to escorting people to a safe house was one hell of a switch around.

"Grab your bags and let's get your mom inside," Adam said gruffly. He strode up to the front door and pushed it open. The house was out of lockdown and he sent a mental thank you to the eye in the sky that was trailing their every move. He didn't have to check the inside. If there had been anyone or indeed anything indoors that shouldn't be then Sanctuary ops would have stopped entry and warned them.

Josh and Maggie were next and Lee brought up the rear. He still had his gun drawn. He always had been the cautious one. When everyone stood in the open hallway Adam approached the small keypad on the wall and entered a code. Lockdown was immediate. Bolts shot and windows locked. Maggie flinched, Josh looked resigned and Lee curious. Jeez, he bet Lee was going to ask questions. He was never happier than when Josh asked where Maggie could lie down.

Adam brushed past Lee and indicated a corridor. "I don't know what's down there. Pick a room. There are showers and spare clothes of all sizes in the closets."

Josh guided his mom down a corridor and took the first door on the right but he didn't stay in there with her. He moved with purpose towards them and Adam dreaded what was coming next. Questions. Demands. It was always the same. He braced himself but was surprised when Josh moved past them to the small kitchen.

"I need coffee. Is there coffee in these places?" Josh was opening and shutting doors. Each cupboard was full to bursting with dried goods and cans and finally with a triumphant "yes" coffee was located. Only instant, nothing fancy, it was enough to distract Lee who joined Josh in the kitchen to help.

Everyone was occupied and Adam turned in a half circle to gauge where everything would be. There was a flight of stairs leading up from the hallway and he took them two at a time eager to find the comms room and to check in with Ops.

The place where the computer and communication hub was housed was smaller than what he was used to in other safe houses. However, it was at the front of the attic space and the wall of trees outside the small window was pretty reassuring. The forest was threatening to encroach on the house and it served to block anything that could approximate a view. Lee had asked about the place being obvious. With Manny's blocking systems and various other under the table processes houses like this one, old holiday homes, were proving to be perfect safe houses.

He logged in to the system and booked himself in. Immediately he had access to case files on the Bullens and also temporary folders for both Maggie and Josh. He opened the one on Maggie and was relieved when it showed no known medical history. From the dates and notes she seemed like the perfect cop's wife and there in black and white was the fact that she had turned down witness protection. The file on Josh was a little fuller but other than the academic stuff, there was little about the man himself. A couple of family photos were in each file. He looked closely at the man at the center of all of this, Gareth Headley, and pulled the photo out to sit it on the surface next to a photo of Alastair.

Was it possible to bring to an end to the years of organized crime and to finally bring Alastair Bullen to justice? He checked who was assigned to this safe house; knew it wouldn't be him. Jennifer Sweeney. He smiled; she was a cool person to know. Handy with her fists and as quick with her mind, she was a friend. They'd worked a case before and he knew Maggie and Josh would be in safe hands.

"Do we have an ETA on Jennifer?" he asked as soon as he connected to Ops.

"She's coming in from one of our west coast houses, she'll be with you mid-morning."

"Josh Headley is talking about a boyfriend—can we put a heads up to him to warn him to keep safe? Then let me know."

"Do we have a name?" Adam thought back to some of what Josh had said in the car. He may have looked like he was concentrating solely on driving but he had heard enough from the back.

"Eric, I don't have a surname, I can get one if you need one. I know he's a lawyer."

"On it. I'll track him down; let you know if I need more info."

"Also. We need to get in and see Gareth Headley now. I'm scanning the notebook we recovered from his wife. It's not big but it has dates and names. Manny will probably be able to match some of this up. None of it means anything without Gareth. With his son and wife safe we have leverage to get information and maybe persuade him to talk."

"Jake is arranging a meet. Anything else?"

"Nothing."

"You know where we are." The disembodied voice was an operative's only connection to the outside world when in lockdown. The support was reassuring. What they had said though, that Jennifer wouldn't be with them until tomorrow, meant one night in the safe house where he could do nothing except sleep. That sounded good.

"What now?" Lee said from the doorway. Adam didn't have to wonder how long he had been standing there. He had heard him arrive about the same time he connected with Ops.

"We wait for the meet to be arranged, for another Sanctuary operative to relieve us here and then we go and see Gareth."

"He's stayed quiet for this long. We can't expect him to suddenly agree to give evidence."

"We have his family and they are safe."

With this Adam logged off of the computer and deliberately waited until Lee moved aside before going downstairs. Lee followed him with yet another one of his patented disappointed sighs and Adam stopped dead on the fourth stair from the bottom. Very carefully he turned to face Lee who had no choice but to stop.

"Whatever you have against me, whatever shit you have in your head that you think I did, you leave it all outside this place." Adam gestured around him. "People who need us need somewhere safe and calm. They do not need pseudo cops with sticks up their asses blathering on about how Sanctuary isn't as good as their beloved FBI." Lee opened his mouth to answer and then shut it again. Adam concluded his warning had been heeded, and he turned sharply to take the remaining stairs to the living room.

Josh sat cross-legged on the sofa. He looked much younger than his twenty-five years.

"Mom says she's going to try sleeping," he said softly.

"Good idea." Adam crouched in front of Josh. "Is there anything you need?"

"Me?" Josh looked confused. "No, I'm fine."

"I'm sorry you had to go without talking to your boyfriend."

Josh shrugged, "'S okay. I know the kind of life I should be living. I was fooling myself thinking I could have anything else. The day my dad killed that girl, no—way back when he did whatever made him Bullen's pet cop—that was the day I wasn't going to have normal."

Adam didn't like the acceptance in Josh's voice, nor the sheen of tears in his eyes. The man had given up everything to do this. His job, his lover and any sense of normalcy. "When we get him behind bars maybe you can get back some of that life."

Josh quirked a smile. He really was a

gorgeous guy. Ordinarily he would have ticked every single one of Adam's boxes. Slim, shorter than Adam, green eyes and dark haired. In a way he reminded Adam of a younger Lee. The thought of that twisted like a knife in his chest. Were he and Lee ever this young and why did being thirty-two make him feel so damn old?

"I wanted to be a cop like my dad, but he always said he wanted me somewhere I could help the little guy, the kid with no choices or the guy who was stuck in a corner. I never imagined for one minute he was talking about himself with that last one. I was never going to do either. School showed I was good at science. Hell, all that studying and it's wasted." He laughed softly, "I'm thinking I need to reevaluate my options here."

"Not always a bad thing, Josh, to have the decision in your hands."

"Yeah," Josh huffed a low laugh and grabbed at Adam's hand that rested next to his thigh on the sofa. He gripped it hard and Adam gripped back. The people he looked after in these safe houses, they just needed a connection that spoke of safety and reassurance. He was being deadly serious with Lee when he had said that. Lee himself was hovering just out of Adam's peripheral vision. His brooding presence made everything here so much more difficult.

"Don't think for a minute that me and Mom thought Dad was anything other than a criminal," Josh began earnestly. "We didn't understand what he did or why. We hated it but I just wanted to keep her alive."

"Your mom is safe now." Adam couldn't imagine the fear of looking over your shoulder twenty-four-seven; if just for that, Alastair Bullen needed a smack down.

Josh released the grip on Adam's hand. "Thank you. I'm going to grab a room and some sleep." He gestured behind him at the corridor with the bedroom doors. "Sort myself out." He looked over Adam's shoulder at what he imagined was the hovering Lee.

"I think the Fed wants to talk to you," Josh said with a smile

"He can wait." Adam couldn't help but return Josh's smile. It was infectious.

Adam stood and extended a hand to help Josh to his feet. As Josh turned to leave he evidently had one last question. "Be honest about something. You're not a cop, are you?"

Adam shook his head and shrugged. "I'm a bodyguard of sorts."

"Okay." Josh didn't say anything else. He simply picked up a cup of coffee from the small table next to the sofa and made his way down the corridor selecting door two as his particular home away from home.

"You need to leave him alone," Lee said firmly.

"What the hell do you mean by that?"

Adam had half an idea what Lee was harping on about but that didn't mean he was going to let the other man know that.

"He's vulnerable." Lee stepped forward. Adam copied the movement which put them near toe to toe in this small room.

"I know."

"Holding hands with the guy? What was that?"

"You're jealous?" Adam couldn't believe the tone in Lee's voice. Lee was actually commenting on how Adam did his job? What the hell?

"Fuck you, Brooke." Lee narrowed his gaze and crossed his arms over his chest. "Don't fuck him over. Like you… shit, Adam."

"Like I fucked you over you mean?" Adam completed the aborted sentence. His breath stilled in his lungs and his stomach heaved at the sorrow that settled in the pit of it. Nothing else mattered than hearing what Lee was going to say back. Lee said nothing. He just set his lips in a stubborn mutinous line and pushed past Adam to get to the kitchen.

"I need a fucking drink."

The computer screen filled the room with an eerie glow as it churned through the pages of information Manny was collating back at Sanctuary Ops. Adam liked the little guy with his glasses and his brilliance and the edge of a complicated tattoo that disappeared under his collar. He was irreverent and snarky, clever and innocent, all wrapped up in about five foot eight inches. He was also scarily good with guns and where that had come from for a computer geek was anyone's guess. Most Sanctuary operatives had back stories. Nik Valentinov had been invalided out of the FBI, Dale MacIntyre was an ex-SEAL and as for Kayden? Well, he was some kind of freaky ninja-trained kid with a past, although you would never be told any of it.

Jake Callahan himself had seen enough in his life to make him sink every penny he had into Sanctuary but Manny gave nothing away about his own past.

"Is that it?" Adam asked tiredly.

Manny's perpetually cheerful voice echoed down the line. "We're about ninety-five percent. It's looking good."

"What do you have so far?"

"Definite matches with the police reports that Beckett got from Alastair's computer to the list of names and dates in Gareth Headley's notebook. Some recurring notes and names. I'm running them through databases as I find them."

"Is it enough to take to the DA?" That was what this was all about; links and notes that made the case against Alastair watertight.

"I'm thinking only Headley's testimony will tip this," Manny offered. "Jake messaged me he's pulled strings with that FBI liaison guy and between them they've moved him to a solitary wing straight from the hospital wing. He's there tomorrow. I'll mail details. Okay one hundred percent in five... four... three... wait... okay I have it all."

"We're out of here as soon as Jennifer arrives."

"I'll make sure you get this analysis in full."

Adam glanced at the clock, it was one am and the house was quiet. Josh and his mom hadn't come out of their respective rooms and after a mostly silent preparation of toast and jam Lee had taken the first room on the left at around eleven. "Go to bed, Manny."

"Will soon," Manny confirmed cheerfully and then signed off. Manny appeared to be perpetually awake. Tiredly Adam stretched and yawned. Logging out he left the attic space room and made his way to the kitchen. Coffee had kept him going so far but, hell, today, or strictly yesterday, had been too much of a mind fuck for his liking. Lee back in his life in such a dramatic way, an extraction based on an adrenaline-fuelled reaction. Jeez, that was one day he was happy to consign to the 'hopefully never happening again' bin. His stomach reminded him he hadn't eaten since they stopped at the gas station and rummaging he located a bag of cookies. Cookies and hot chocolate and bed sounded like a good thing to be doing.

Finally under the covers he considered safe house eight. Small, but adequate, not for a family maybe, but it was secure, remote, and had a feel of the safe house he had spent so long in up over the border in Mirabel in Canada. He didn't fall asleep quickly. He never did in a strange place. Unconsciously his hand travelled south and closed around his dick. More comfort than anything as his head was too screwed to imagine puling one off now. Fucking Lee and the confusion and anxiety that his presence brought to the table. His dick went from soft to semi hard in seconds as images from the day pushed into his head. This morning, Lee pushed over the table, and the single word the man had uttered as he complied with every push Adam made. *Please.* Releasing the moving hold he had on his dick he deliberately shuffled to lay on his front and turned his head to face away from the door.

He wasn't going to think about his ex-lover but sleep had only just begun to pull him under when Lee's voice broke into his thoughts. He rolled on his back expecting there to be nothing in his room and that Lee's voice was a figment of his imagination. Instead he felt the corner of the bed depress as Lee sat on the end in the dark.

"What the fuck?" Adam bit out. He blinked to accustom himself to the dark. The door was shut and Lee was sitting on his bed in boxers and a T.

"Why?" Lee said softly.

CHAPTER 7

"Go back to bed, Lee." Adam wasn't ready for deep conversation at ass o'clock in the morning. And the whole word why? What was that?

"I'm not going back to bed until you tell me," Lee said. His tone was so damn matter of fact; like telling him the truth wasn't going to rip his world apart. Adam considered the question. He wasn't ready to do this with Lee. They had a case to concentrate on.

"You've had over a year since you lost the right to know anything about me."

"Tell me why."

Adam pushed at the covers until he sat upright. Lee had one leg drawn up under him and his hands rested on his thighs. He looked relaxed but Adam couldn't see the expression on Lee's face let alone read the intent in his eyes.

"Why what?"

"Why did you do it? Why did you take a bribe to disrupt the chain of evidence in the Robertson case? If I understood it then maybe we could get past it; go back to being friends."

Adam knew this would happen eventually. Lee and him in an enclosed space would never equal calm. And friends? They were never just friends. "Funny," he huffed with a sarcastic laugh. "You never once asked me why." Adam leaned over and turned on the bedside light. If this was really going down then there needed to be a little light on the subject.

Lee rocked backward. "Shit Adam, I didn't know I had to." He shook his head. "I guess I imagined you would just tell me what was going on."

"And I never *imagined* I would have to explain. Maybe to the guys who paid my wages, but not to you. You saw those photos and from that moment you weren't able to even look at me let alone listen to me. I needed you to trust I was doing the right thing. Is that so hard to understand?"

"What? You wanted blind trust from me when all the evidence said you were screwing us over?"

Adam paused and considered what he was going to say. The day he had been called into the office, shown the photos and asked to explain himself had been the hardest and easiest of days. Pissed that he had been caught, and inwardly feeling screwed, it was the outside face that he showed to colleagues that was the easiest. His expression would show he didn't care he was being hauled over the coals. His face would show that it didn't matter Lee saw the images. "You stood there in that room, Lee, and you looked at me differently. After all those years of being your partner, your lover, you refused to think anything except the worst."

"I didn't know what to say. I was working the internal leak—you know that. We knew someone in that office was bad. Shit, Adam, I was in shock."

"You were in shock? I never thought for one minute I had internal affairs following my every footstep."

"I didn't know they were—"

"I'm supposed to believe that 'wonder-boy Myers' wasn't one hundred percent in the loop in his own fucking department?"

"I wasn't—"

"Think whatever you want Lee. It was obvious to even an idiot that the pictures, whoever took the damn things, weren't faked. When you looked at them you made a decision your head could live with."

"I didn't have a choice; I had a job to do." The frustration in Lee's voice was intense.

Adam leaned back against the pillows. This was possibly one of the most surreal experiences he had ever been part of. In every dream he had where Lee confronted him about those final days with the FBI Adam always played it cool. He had all the answers and he could cut Lee out of his life with nothing more than a *fuck you*. Lee hadn't believed him, believed in him, therefore he was dead to Adam. Thing is, this wasn't exactly going to plan.

"So tell me what the photos meant, tell me why I was wrong."

"I'm not ready to go back there." Adam couldn't keep the frustration from his voice. There was so much tension sparking off around them and not all of it good. Now was not the right time to be considering things long past.

"I loved you, Adam. You only had to explain, but you said nothing." Lee pushed a hand through his short blond hair in frustration and it stood up briefly before gravity took over on the silky locks.

Adam could remember how soft it was to the touch. How he loved to grasp Lee and twist his fingers in Lee's hair as they kissed. His dick filled at the thought. The sex had always been so damn good.

"You thought you loved me," he finally said. Just for something to say really; to break the silence. "I'm not having this conversation. You need to leave." *You need to leave before I go against everything I think and drag you into the bed.* He focused on remembering the day Lee had stood by and done nothing when accusations flew. That stilled the arousal in his body but not enough to completely erase it.

"So if I said sorry, if I said I wanted to listen? Can you make me see why I was wrong?" Lee offered gently.

Everything was there in front of Adam. Lee in his room, on his bed, the slim blond moving up toward the headboard as Adam decided what to say. There was such concentration in Lee's expression, coupled with expectation. It would be so easy to push the covers away and take what he wanted at this moment because he had been without for so long. Mesmerized, he leaned forward as Lee moved and they were so close. Adam could hear the rush of his blood, the need that was building up inside.

"Help me see why you broke the law." Lee said gently.

Adam reared back and threw the covers away from him coming up and out of bed in an instant. Just those few words were enough to snap him out of the cloud of need that had built in his head.

"Get out of my room," he snapped forcefully.

Lee stood in a flurry of movement and was right up in Adam's space. "I'm staying until you tell me why you did it."

Adam reached out and twisted his hand into Lee's T-shirt and pulled him closer until nothing more than a breath separated them. "Then you'll be here a long time." They stared at each other for what seemed like ages. Adam couldn't be sure who moved first, whether it was him desperate for touch, or Lee desperate to demand answers. The first touch of lips was hard and punishing and neither gave quarter.

This was easy. This violent taking and wanting was familiar and Adam was pushing Lee away and back to the bed. In a move eerily similar to the one in the office it was Lee who was facedown on the bed and Adam rutting against him. He didn't want to look Lee in the eye and Lee wasn't stopping him. He could have. He was strong enough.

They always had roles. Adam was physically bigger, would always be able to lift and push and hold Lee, and normally Lee was happy to be manhandled. Only this time he was a spitting, hissing, writhing mass of demanding need under Adam's hands. Adam wanted to push and feel and hold but it was a battle to touch. A desperate need to learn each other after nothing for so long; to force each other to the limit. Adam had Lee trapped beneath him, his legs stilled by Adam's hold and the only connection was Adam's dick in the crease of Lee's cotton covered ass. Adam gripped Lee's hair, turned his head, and stole a brutal tasting battling kiss. Lee swore in the kiss, but there was no heat. It was a plea for more.

Adam pulled back, releasing his hold just enough to push Lee's T-shirt up to his neck and pull his boxers down enough to expose the curve of his ass and the promise between. Adam tugged his own shorts down until the hardness of him was against Lee. They had no lube, no condoms, nothing and Adam wasn't going to push inside. Instead he set a punishing pace in the groove of Lee's ass cheeks. Selfishly he wasn't interested in getting Lee off, he just needed to mark this man. He kissed a trail of gentle touches across Lee's broad shoulders and was aware of Lee moving with his hand around his dick. He was whimpering under him, pleading, and Adam was pushed over the edge, coming in heaving strips over Lee's ass and back. He immediately pulled away and Lee rolled over onto his back.

Lee's dick was still hard, his hand stripping the length frantically, his eyes half shut and then with a cry of completion he came over his hand and stomach.

"Fuck you, Adam," Lee immediately snapped as he pulled his T-shirt over his head and used it to wipe himself down.

"It's what you wanted. It's all you ever wanted from me."

Lee didn't rise to the taunt. Instead he focused on the case they had been discussing. "Why did the lawyer give the evidence to you? Why didn't he come to me. Or hell, anyone else on the damn case?"

Adam winced inwardly. Sex hadn't stopped Lee's anger, if anything the temper in his lover was just turning up in heat.

Lee stood and distanced himself from the bed immediately. Adam couldn't meet his gaze. His marks were around Lee's neck, red blooms of need that recalled the path of passion. They never had trouble getting off. "For God's sake," Lee shouted angrily. "Tell me."

Adam bowed his head. Why wasn't he telling Lee? What was stopping him? When it had all happened, the betrayal of losing Lee's complete and utter acceptance was a knife to his belly. Was that stopping him from being rational? Before he knew it every single thing he was keeping from Lee began to bubble to the surface.

"You remember our last case together, the Robertsons and the crooked lawyer and the whole DA fallout." The very lawyer that was photographed handing the parcel to Adam. The parcel that disappeared.

"I can't forget it." Lee snapped, anger

still in his voice.

"The lawyer contacted me off the record, just me, promised he had something for me but that I couldn't tell anyone else."

"So you listened to a lawyer for the other freaking side? You didn't book that meeting in, or tell me. Why?"

"I couldn't." Lee shook his head and anger spiked inside Adam. Who was Lee to stand there and judge Adam for what he had done? "We had spent weeks on that damn case, I was willing to take anything that could break it. The lawyer said he had an account by a witness to the case. The witness gave it to his lawyer and said it was his only protection against losing his life. Ironic really as the witness was shot the next morning which invalidated the whole sorry thing." Adam was lost in memories; as if he was there in that alley way taking the envelope with the contents that would change his life.

"So I ask you again. Why did the lawyer give it to you?"

"He said I was the only one he could get anywhere close to trusting. He was scared and he needed protection and he said the FBI had betrayed him." There was that word again. Betrayed. Adam was seeing that word a lot in his head. "The guy was convinced I would know what to do and what was right."

"What was right was sharing the information with your team," Lee said hotly. "Your work partner, fuck, your life partner. It looked like it was a payoff in all the photos."

"It wasn't a payoff. I destroyed what I was given."

"Did you read what you were given? What did it say?"

"The lawyer was right. It was notes about an FBI leak that connected straight to the DA's office. Dates, names, observations, the complete story. Well, the complete fabrication of a story."

"*The* leak? Our internal leak?"

"No. The lawyer had told me what was in it, but I didn't believe it. I was convinced it was all lies, even after I had read it. It meant nothing."

"How do you know that? What made you think it wasn't about the person that internally has us chasing our tails?"

"Because it named names, Lee. And I knew they were wrong."

Lee sat back on the bed as he visibly deflated. "How can you sit here and tell me the transcript named names about a leak in the freaking FBI and yet you didn't book the evidence in?"

"I couldn't do it."

"Why?" Lee sounded so confused. And damn it, there was that why again. Lee wasn't going to leave this room without accepting Adam had a reason. He gazed straight into Lee's eyes. What he was going to say wasn't easy to hear. Finally he couldn't not say it.

"Because the person named in the account was you."

Lee stood immediately with denial cut deep in his face. "My name? I wasn't—"

"See, Lee," Adam said tiredly, "I destroyed it because I knew it was lies. I didn't even think about it. And you know why I didn't believe it?"

"Why?"

"Because I loved you and I trusted you and I never believed for one minute you could betray the Bureau or betray me."

CHAPTER 8

Lee felt sick. He had exited the room as soon as the words left Adam's lips and locked himself in the bathroom of his own room. He attempted to analyze what he was feeling. Anger, regret, shame, and the awful realization that at some point when it all hit the fan at the Bureau, both he and Adam had been manipulated.

Information implicating Lee in the public arena would have led to his dismissal and arrest. Whether the information had been real or not, the damage would have been done. Adam had taken the fall for Lee and all Adam had had in return from his supposed lover was to be dropped like a hot potato.

The knock on the door was expected. Adam would not let it lie and have Lee hiding in a freaking bathroom. He had tried to stop him leaving the bedroom but Lee still had some moves on his larger lover.

"Lee?"

A mix of self-pity, shame, and grief spun in his head and he swallowed before answering "I'll be out in a minute—"

"Ops called, Jennifer is twenty minutes out." Lee heard the words and waited for the noise of Adam moving away. He held his breath until finally Adam walked away from the door. Lee wasn't ready to face him. Shit.

In a daze he stood in front of the mirror blindly looking at the man who stared back at him. Gently he touched the red marks on his collarbone. Adam took him out of who he really was, he always had the touch to make Lee just *feel*. Those photos had been so damn incriminating. He'd not long joined the FBI version of internal affairs, a newbie, he'd only really worked his way through one case and having evidence of Adam handed to him on a plate was damning. He thought back to the day that Sean had called him to one side.

"I'm sorry, Lee," he had begun. Lee wasn't sure how to take Sean or the tone in his voice. "I know you and Adam are close," the man had added. When Lee opened the envelope he hadn't believed what he had seen. Of course he hadn't seen betrayal, or payoffs, he had just seen photos of Adam doing something that he hadn't shared with Lee. Then to be told Adam was suspected of taking payoffs and bribes? The evidence had been damning. He'd taken action immediately. He'd asked Adam to lunch and they sat and chatted over pizza and hot sweet coffee. Lee didn't remember how he had managed to get through the lunch without being as sick as he felt now. He gave Adam every chance and Adam had said nothing.

Shaking his head clear of memories he started the shower and climbed under the scalding hot water. Jennifer arriving meant it was time for Adam and him to visit the prison in which Headley senior was incarcerated. That was at least something they could concentrate on. He needed to get back in the game and try to push the other shit to one side. Wrapped in a towel he left the bathroom and walked into his room. It didn't surprise him to see Adam sat on the bed waiting. The huge man looked small somehow with his elbows resting on his knees and his chin on his steepled fingers.

Lee stopped. God. He wished he knew what to say. Sorry wasn't going to cut it. He took the step forward to be in Adam's reach. What he expected he didn't know. Maybe Adam would punch him, maybe he would ignore him. Whatever he did at least it would be *something*.

Adam lifted his head and reached out with his hands to settle his palms on Lee's towel wrapped ass. With a pull from Adam he stumbled that last little bit of distance. Adam turned his face and pressed his cheek against the damp skin above the towel and Lee grasped

Adam's head with both hands, pressing him closer.

Slowly Adam moved to place a gentle kiss just above Lee's navel and it was too much. Lee sank to his knees between Adam's legs and waited. So many words spun around them but it appeared neither man could actually grasp enough to form a coherent responsive sentence. Adam leaned down the final inch, Lee pulled in by the spark of anticipation, the echoes of the sudden and intense lust still suspended between them, and they touched lips. It was heat, it was a connection, and Lee shut his eyes, angling his head just to feel more of Adam's soft lips as they pressed a slick of warmth against his. This felt so right, so perfect. Why the hell had he ever let this go?

Adam's breath was warm against Lee's lips, and he stole another kiss feeling Adam's hands curl at the back of his neck digging into his hair and pulling him up on his knees for the kiss. Adam started to talk then between kisses, each word carried through touch, a gentle smoothing of fingers down Lee's arms, seeing each fine hair stand in a shiver, moving his fingers onto his chest, exploring gently, desperate to touch each inch.

"It's out there now," he said simply.

"Will we ever get past this?"

"Past two stubborn idiots losing years of being together? I want to." Adam whispered into the brightening room as Lee relaxed back into Adam's hold. He tightened his fingers on Adam's hip, firm against the bone, marking the skin stretched there, the breath in his lungs caught in a sudden panic. They were so far apart, the Fed and the bodyguard, Lee back to the Bureau when this finished, Adam to God knows where, doing God knows what.

Lee took a deep breath and he could feel Adam tensing against him at the hesitation in his voice, until he said all he could say now... all he could give Adam…

"I'm sorry."

Adam pulled back and nodded. "You need to get dressed." He pointed this out with a gentle touch of his hand to Lee's bare chest. Lee tensed and leaned into the man who was so dramatically back in his life. "I'll make coffee."

Lee opened the closet and glanced in at the racks of clothes ranging from baby clothes to suits and ties. It was a bulging space and he pushed aside the girl clothes and pulled out a soft blue Tee and a gray hoodie. Further exploration found him jeans that while not fitting perfectly were okay with a belt. The T-shirt was warm against his skin and the fleeced jacket was soft.

At least dressed he had that one further layer of protection. Hefting his gun he checked it over and then slid it into the space between the base of his back and his jeans.

Stretching tall he caught sight of himself

in the mirror. Red marks bloomed on his neck just above the Tee but with a subtle pull of the material in the hoodie he could hide most of it. Not that he wanted to. Perversely, he wanted everyone to see Adam's marks of possession on his skin. It just wasn't the professional thing to do.

Sighing he checked the room one last time and then, closing the closet door, he left to join his lover in the main room.

Jennifer was nothing like Lee expected. Tall and Amazonian she was not. In fact she probably topped five-eight in heels and had hair the color of corn silk to her waist. She wore a black dress covered in faux diamonds and it wasn't much of a dress, more like two pieces of material she had been sewn into. Lee may be gay but, hell, even he could see she was one sexy but completely impractical babe.

"Shower first," she grumbled as she

removed impossibly high heeled shoes and kicked them into the corner of the living room. Her vowels were pure accented French. "I tell you, this is screwing with my head. Ambassador's party at the embassy and then straight on to the ass end of the forest. No down time. Jake so owes me one."

"The extraction was unplanned," Adam said with a laugh in his voice. Pouting scarlet lips she nearly climbed Adam to plant a sticky red kiss on his mouth leaving a generous smear of red.

"Anything for you, gorgeous," Jennifer simpered.

Lee pushed down the irrational spike of jealousy. Adam was not bi. He was gay and women didn't do it for him. She crossed to Lee with a thoughtful expression on her face and traced a scarlet-tipped nail down his chest.

"And who do we have here?"

"Lee Myers, FBI," Lee introduced

himself quickly. Jennifer's eyes widened at this tidbit of information but she said nothing. She brushed past him and waited at the start of the corridor.

"Which one?" she asked. Was it his imagination or was the French accent lessening the more she spoke?

"Second left. Usual choice of clothes in the closet." Adam chuckled.

Lee narrowed his gaze as she sashayed down to Adam's room. As soon as the door shut Lee couldn't hold back his reaction.

"We're leaving her in charge of the Headleys?" It seemed impossible to think the vamp with the lips and the legs up to her tits could be of any use. Surely all that hair would get in the way, and the nails, and fuck... the heels.

Adam shrugged but he had a smile on his face. Lee wanted to register his protest but Josh came out of his bedroom yawning widely.

"Whad'I'miss?" He slurred the words on another yawn.

"Your operative arrived," Adam explained. "She'll be assigned to you until we know what's happening."

"Oh?" Josh said curiously. "Where?"

"She's just showering off her last case. Coffee?"

All three men sat at the small counter with coffee and Lee's irritation and worry grew as Jennifer had yet to emerge from Adam's bedroom. She was probably in there checking her nails or some equally useless shit. His worries and fears about Sanctuary returned to the surface. Did they really know what they were doing?

When the door opened and she emerged, some twenty minutes after going in, it wasn't just Lee who stared.

Gone was the vamp in the little black dress and in its place was Jennifer with her hair braided and held back off of her face in some kind of complicated looped and tightly-in-place design. Her face was devoid of makeup and she wore loose fitting jeans, a simple sweatshirt, and western style boots on her feet. She had a weapon in her hands and checked the safety before sliding it into a shoulder holster.

"Fuck," she swore succinctly. Every single cultured French syllable had disappeared and in its place was pure Brooklyn. "I need coffee."

Adam poured her a cup of steaming black caffeine and after she sipped the burning hot brew she extended a hand to Josh. Lee noted, as Josh grasped her hand, that the long red nails had gone.

"Josh Headley?" she asked."Jennifer Cohen. I'll be your bodyguard for the duration."

Lee glanced at Adam who was staring in his direction. The bastard was laughing at him.

CHAPTER 9

Adam didn't imagine Lee was having any more of an easy time handling what had happened back at the safe house than he was. They were both quiet in the car although Lee kept looking his way. Adam couldn't help but see the movement out of the corner of his eye. There was no talking though so he was thankful that he was able to use the time to concentrate on the driving.

They were twenty minutes away from the prison just before lunch time and as they weren't allowed in to see Gareth Headley until two, Adam took the initiative and pulled into a diner parking lot. Food and talk were both on his to-do list. They settled in a corner booth and after a silent and short battle of wills Adam sat facing the door. The menu was simple and the selections easy. As soon as the order was filled Adam knew where they should start but he didn't immediately launch into anything. He looked at Lee who was slumped in his chair and tracing patterns on the table top with his finger. He appeared thoughtful and Adam considered that they were thinking about the same thing. Were they both on the job or was Lee introspective after last night? The drinks arrived and Adam sipped hot coffee as he waited for Lee to say something. Anything.

"Are you thinking what I'm thinking?" Lee finally said.

"I don't know," Adam moved in his seat and leaned into the corner. The table was a little close to the seats and fixed with a bar. It made someone of his height and width a little claustrophobic. Still, he wouldn't change anything for the clear view of all the exits. "What were you thinking about?"

"The case," Lee offered with a frown. He pulled a notebook from his pocket and placed it flat on the table.

"Someone compromised the FBI safe house where Morgan Drake was being held. We know for a fact there's been an agency leak back at the Bureau. What if we hypothesize there is a connection. That whoever the leak is, is working for the Bullens?"

Adam pulled his cell out of his pocket and thumbed through his emails. The message received early this morning from Manny was the one he wanted to show Lee. He turned it around to face his partner. "Manny sent over the list of matches from the notes that Maggie Headley had to the case files that were taken from Gregory Bullen's PC. There are two pairs of letters which repeat but Manny can't match them. They appear enough to make them worthy of notice and the last notification of one of the sets of initials was the day before Elisabeth Costain was shot in the alley."

"Which letters?" Lee was sliding the screen to read down the list and then he stopped as he reached halfway. He looked up at Adam but there was no sense of recognition in his expression. He carried on scrolling to the bottom.

"SH and EC. Those are the letters we can't match to reports," Adam summarized. "However, EC seems to tie in with Elisabeth Costain."

"That would make sense."

"SH is the initial that appears last. What if that is the person inside the FBI?"

"That's a reach."

"It's the only lead we have."

"SH? Sean Hanson?" Lee immediately concluded exactly what Adam had thought. "The agent working as liaison between Sanctuary and the Bureau? There must be a hundred men working with the FBI with those initials. Hell, Adam, he's one of the good guys."

"Agreed with the hundreds of matches. But, it may be worth seeing if there are any correlations between the initials and agents and staff involved or connected with the Bullen case."

"Or with you and me," Lee said softly.

"You're thinking there is some connection between you, me, the Bullens and the leak?" Adam considered the suggestion. "Stranger things have happened," he finally concluded.

"All I'm saying is that last case you worked, Lloyd Robertson. Is it possible that he was linked to the Bullens? Lloyd ran money schemes for a lot of very shady people. Who's to say he wasn't the Bullens' money man. We could get your guy, Manny, to see what he can track down. It was the Lloyd Robertson case that was compromised by your actions—your alleged actions." He corrected himself even as he said it. Then he ducked his head in a slight show of embarrassment.

"I was close to shutting Robertson down

then he was shot and killed—"

"I remember. We woke up to the news on CNN." Lee went quiet.

Adam could see Lee was remembering their last morning together before the shit hit the fan.

"And then you were framed," Lee added, "and I didn't see it."

Adam wanted to grab Lee's hand and hold it tight; he sounded so resigned. They were both to blame. He didn't though, as he wasn't sure how that would go down in this small diner. The two men could handle anything but the last thing they wanted was to attract attention.

"I shouldn't have placed that responsibility on you to accept what you saw as lies. I'm not sure if it had been you that I wouldn't have doubted the same way."

"You didn't though. You believed in me, knew it wasn't me who was the FBI mole."

"Can we leave it? The whole blame thing?" Adam leaned forward in his seat when sadness passed over Lee's face. "That's not to say not talk about it, ever. I just mean for the next short time while we get our visit over with Gareth Headley."

"I can do that." Lee nodded. "Hell, when this is over we go our own ways anyway."

Adam didn't want that. He wanted to talk, he wanted to fix this, hell he wanted to get over his own insecurities so he could look at Lee and not feel disappointed at the other man's actions. "Why did you ask to work with me, Lee? You knew I didn't want you anywhere near me, and you still thought…"

"Sean asked me to, and I didn't have to think about it. I wanted to see you." Lee shrugged then looked down at the paper. "Can you get your team to run the check on the initials?"

Lee evidently wanted to change the

subject and Adam was strangely enough very cool with that. Despite having questions the last thing he wanted really was an in-depth discussion on his love life where anyone could hear.

"You want this done outside of the Bureau."

"No sense in raising red flags."

Adam tabbed to Manny's number and connected almost immediately.

"Yo, big man," Manny answered.

"Manny, can you do a check on any agents with those initials S and H from maybe ten years back to today that may connect with the organized crime team, the Bullens, with me or Agent Lee Myers, or with the last case I worked at the Bureau?"

"Which was?" Manny was typing even as he was talking.

"Robertson, the Bullens' money man, murdered just over two years ago."

"FBI as a whole, too many hits."

"How about narrowing it to the organized crime team past and present?" Lee suggested. "Makes sense for the Bullens to want someone on the inside where it mattered."

"Running. Okay, we have twenty-six hits, ten female, sixteen male. Factor in the Bullens and that drops to ten. Add in your office brings it down to four. That's as far as I can take it down."

"What are the names?" Adam gestured for the notebook and a pen and Lee slid them across the table. Adam scribbled them down and heard the momentary pause before Sean Hanson's name.

"Look, Adam, this name came up on my matches. Should we be giving a heads-up to Jake? The man is Jake's shadow for nigh on half the day."

"Leave it for now. I'm running the names past Lee. I only recognize one and that's Sean and that is only because we met yesterday. Lee may know more."

"I'll be here." Manny signed off with his customary "laters".

Lee took the pad from Adam and turned the paper around. "Sarah Harrison, she's on maternity leave, spent most of last year practicing her new surname after marrying John Harrison in accounts. Selina Hernandez, she's a good field agent. Mostly out of the LA office but I know she was seconded to our office just after you left. Simon Hatfield, he's this new guy, fresh out of Quantico, and then Sean Hanson. I don't know a lot about him personally but he's working hard at getting Sanctuary looked on as something more than a renegade organization."

"Jake would love that. Renegade," Adam smiled. The idea of his thoughtful ticking-boxes boss being anything like a kind of renegade was something he couldn't see.

Their food arrived and suddenly they

had something to focus on other than the case. Lee was still talking about the people they had identified with the initials SH. They could be barking up entirely the wrong tree with this SH. Just because the letters featured in Headley's list and appeared to tie up with each case didn't mean it was pointing at an FBI contact.

Listening to Lee talk was therapeutic. Adam worked through his thoughts quietly until the smile he gave when Lee cracked a joke about procedure was actually genuine. He'd forgotten just how much he liked to hear Lee talk. He enjoyed the softer tone of his voice and the clipped preppy accent that sounded every vowel he had. He remembered Lee's voice loud with passion and soft with teasing and he realized why it had hurt so much when he had lost Lee's trust. He missed Lee. He missed his voice and his teasing and his body and his hair. Fuck. Everything.

"Ready?" Lee was saying. It broke

through Adam's thoughts and the question startled him. "You spaced out there, big guy."

"Yeah." He glanced at his watch. "Let's hit the road."

"Just gonna use the bathroom," Lee said and slid out of his seat. "Meet you at the car."

Adam paid the check and left the diner. The day was warm and the road busy. He crossed to the car and leaned against it, raising his face to the sun. No point in wasting the heat. His cell vibrated and he answered without checking the screen.

"Something else came up," Manny dived in without preliminaries.

"What?"

"I don't know if this is of any use but you know that Fed you're with? Lee Myers. I'm turning up some connections between him and one of the people on the list and I don't mean work connections."

"What kind of connections?"

"A joint address for part of last year but not on their personnel files. I dug quite a lot deeper than the normal sweep for information. Looks to me like your Fed was sharing a place with our very own Sean Hanson."

Adam said his thanks but could barely hear the words he was saying over the sudden bitterness that flooded him. Sharing a place with one of the names on the list? Why wouldn't Lee immediately tell him that? Fuck, he told Adam about everything else he knew concerning the other people on the list. Right down to that woman practicing her married name on FBI paperwork.

Lee walked out the front door and slipped his shades from his pocket and onto his face. In a gesture similar to Adam's he lifted his face to the sun. But he grimaced. Unlike Adam, Lee was prone to burning and wasn't a great sun worshipper. Suddenly Adam hated that he knew that.

"Why didn't you tell me?" he snapped as soon as Lee reached him.

"Tell you what?" Lee said frowning. Adam wished he could see Lee's blue eyes to check for deceit.

"You and Sean Hanson."

"Oh."

"Is that all you can say? You're fucking one of the suspects in a case and you don't think it's important to share with me?" Abruptly all the warm fuzziness of smiling at each other in the diner flew out of the window. A mask fell over Lee's face as suddenly as the bars on the windows in a safe house lock-down.

"I don't have to tell you everything I did for two years, Adam," Lee said stubbornly. He crossed his arms over his chest.

"You fucked a suspect," Adam bit out angrily.

"Like I was fucking you when you were breaking the law?" Lee snapped back equally as pissed off. Then he immediately deflated and leaned back against the car next to Adam. "Shit, Adam, I didn't mean that. I wasn't sleeping with Sean. He needed a place to stay so I gave him my spare room. That's all. And he wasn't a freaking suspect when that happened. He was just a friend in need."

"Okay." Adam walked around to the driver's side and unlocked the doors. He climbed in, had his belt on, and was starting the engine before Lee even opened his door.

"Adam—" he started.

"Forget it." Adam was pissed and he wasn't entirely convinced about why he was losing his cool. Jealousy? Frustration? Sadness? Any and all of these were spinning around inside him. He didn't own Lee. Their relationship had ended two years ago and Lee was perfectly okay to sleep with whomever he wanted to.

"There hasn't been anyone, okay?" Lee

said tiredly. He removed his sunglasses and pressed at his temples with his fingers. He was staring at Adam and his blue eyes were filled with emotion. "Not since you."

"Just you and your right hand?" Adam finally said. Then he quirked a smile which, thankfully, Lee returned. Adam reached for the satnav and typed in the zip code they needed. The disembodied voice instructed them to turn around when possible. It was enough to break the weird feeling of connection in the car. Adam didn't want to spend any more time imagining Lee being fucked in his bed by the tall dark Sean Hanson. Lee said nothing happened. That they were just friends. Adam trusted him.

He pulled out of the car park and into the stream of traffic.

There would be time to work through the shit in his head later.

CHAPTER 10

Coxsackie Correctional Facility, generally known as Coxsackie, held about a thousand men.

Lee only knew this because his smart phone told him so. Wikipedia wasn't much of a resource with only a few paragraphs on the prison itself. Still it was enough to get a feel for what he should expect and it wasn't the first prison he had been inside of. They left I87 and headed east passing a bank, some kind of budget motel, and a few dollar stores. Not exactly the best introduction to the area but prisons needed a place around them supporting families that probably visited from all over. Cheap accommodation for visitors already under the strain of having a loved one inside was a given right close to the prison.

"Stop feeling sorry for them," Adam said grumpily.

"I'm not," Lee lied. Adam saw things in black and white. You were good or bad. There wasn't a middle ground. No, that wasn't strictly true; when you got to know Adam you saw the multitude of layers that made the man. Lee had seen the inside of his lover. It hurt that he was getting the black and white version now. Cursing inwardly he wished for a lot of things to change. That he hadn't believed accusations against the man he loved and that he hadn't offered Sean a place to stay when he had lost his apartment after a fire last year. Just for a few seconds in the diner he had imagined there was something there between them. A spark of memory that could potentially turn into something much more again. Then Sean happened. Clearly when he had been in the head Adam had been handed the information tying Sean to Lee and wasn't that just the best thing to happen all day.

"You are. There's a reason these guys are

here—"

"Leave it, Adam," was all he managed to say. Adam had always teased him about the statistics of repeat offenders and the social reasons that some crimes were perpetrated. Lee had all that at his fingertips; part and parcel of his sociology and criminology degree. Adam wasn't teasing this time though. There was a thread of bitterness in his voice and it hurt. If he was in Adam's head he imagined he would see resentment and, hell, Lee couldn't blame Adam one bit. He spoke so eloquently about miscarriages of justice and could spout information to support his trust going back twenty or thirty years. Yet, one photo and he couldn't see past his own pain to what could be behind it.

Shit.

Adam pulled into a long drive between two expanses of neatly kept grass and suddenly Coxsackie, in all its Prison Break glory, was standing in front of them. The bell-tower and weather vane stood tall above the administration building. Lee knew there had been a bell inside there until recently—Wikipedia said so. The car park divided into two sides and Adam pulled left and found a spot under a wide oak for shade.

Saying nothing, both men left the car and walked the short distance to the center and the gate itself. After displaying their credentials and being checked from a list they were met by a sour faced officer who escorted them through the initial gated and fenced area. The wire and mesh were three deep for strength and formed a somewhat sinister canopy above them. Light still filtered through the lacework but every so often it was blocked when the metal met in frequent flat, oblong catchments. Razor wire in wicked curves rose from the latticework and Lee felt as closed in as it was possible to be. He hated these places.

The officer had them sign in at the reception and then they moved through metal scanners and were finally patted down. All of this was completed in utter silence and only then were they allowed through to the first section of the interior. Locked gates opened and then closed behind them and the gray metal and brick became a long tunnel that finally widened out into a larger anteroom.

"Wait here," the officer said perfunctorily. He disappeared through double doors and Lee stood alone with Adam.

"You okay?" Adam asked.

Lee shot him a confused look. He hadn't expected Adam to talk let alone ask him that. Only Adam had seen inside Lee's head, heard Lee talk about visiting his dad in a place like this, of the metal and the gray and the oppression and the sheer hell of being a small kid. The Bureau knew his dad was a career criminal who had died in a prison not dissimilar to this one when Lee was only eleven. That was common knowledge. What wasn't common to all was the scars it had left on Lee.

"I hate these places," Lee murmured.

Adam placed a hand on his arm and Lee consciously leaned into the touch, letting Adam know he valued the concern. Appreciated it, yes, but Lee was somewhat shocked by the gesture given all the shit that had gone down in the last two days. He glanced sideways at Adam who had dropped his hand and was now busy looking at blank walls. He desperately wanted to say something but just as Adam knew him and how much prisons freaked him out, he knew Adam. Big, brawny Adam and his layers.

"This way, please." The officer had returned and he gestured through the door he had reappeared at. Inhaling and straightening his shoulders Lee followed Adam through the door and the next into a large room. A table and chairs sat in the middle—much like a business conference room only one where the table and chairs were bolted to the floor. Unlike the room he'd used to see his dad in, this one was filled with light that flooded in through the south facing windows. Of course the windows had mesh and bars but still, the view over the acres of prison lands was a beautiful one. Lee felt like this was the cruelest punishment of all, to see so much freedom and have it so close but know you can't touch it.

"Wait here." Evidently the officer was a man of few words.

Lee sat in one of the chairs to wait and Adam selected another at a ninety degree angle to him. The whole meeting would appear more like an informal chat than an interrogation.

Both men turned to face the door as Gareth Headley was ushered in. He wore the bright orange of a prisoner and was handcuffed to the table before being encouraged to sit down. Lee wasn't shocked at the changes in the man. He had seen this before. Gareth's police photos were of a healthy, robust and slightly overweight man with carefully styled steel-gray hair, who had the perfect family life and enthusiasm in his eyes.

This man was smaller somehow, a paler, more ill version of what was in the case file. His gray hair was buzz-cut now and his face marked with cuts and bruises. The officer stood behind him and crossed his arms over his chest.

"Please leave," Adam said. He had used the word please but it was entirely overshadowed by the snapped 'leave'. There was nothing saying a guard had to be there. The room was covered by cameras, the prisoner was locked down, and both he and Adam had federal clearance. The guard said nothing, simply inclined his head and left the room.

And then there were three.

"Mr Headley," Adam offered politely.

Gareth didn't even react to that. Lee

imagined he had seen a lot of federal employees all probably sitting there with intent in their eyes.

"Special agent Lee Myers," Adam indicated Lee, "and I am Adam Brooke." Adam held out a hand to shake but Gareth simply sat and stared. There was a mutinous tightening of his lips but his eyes were devoid of any emotion other than resignation. "We're here to ask you—"

"Ask me what I know. I'll tell you nothing. You can posture and talk. I'll ignore that. Then robo-guard can take me back for the rest of my twenty." That was one hell of a lot of words to spill from Gareth's lips and obviously well rehearsed.

Lee glanced at Adam. They hadn't discussed how they were going to handle this. They had, it seemed, fallen back on old habits. So he expected Adam would be bullish and demanding and for Lee to wait for a moment when he could be the voice of reason. The same pattern had worked on many occasions before.

"We have your wife and son," Adam said plainly.

Lee straightened in his chair. Fuck. That was going to go down like a lead balloon.

Gareth was up and out of his chair in an instant, the chains rattling against the table.

"Sit down, Gareth." Adam's tone brooked no discussion but Gareth had fear in his eyes.

"Why? They don't know anything. They're not involved. You fuckers—"

"Sit down."

"They were safe. Leave them alone—"

"Sit down."

"Why would you have them?"

"Sit down!" Adam said again.

Gareth didn't so much sit as fall into his chair, despair carved into his face.

"I'm from a foundation called Sanctuary.

We provide safe places for people that need them."

"Part of the FBI? The Feds can't help us…" Headley wasn't listening. He was shaking his head from side to side and the fear in him was palpable to Lee.

"Listen to me," Adam ordered loudly. Finally Gareth seemed to focus on Adam. There was a sheen of moisture in the prisoner's eyes and Lee felt a subtle twinge of pity. He hoped Adam got the hell on with explaining. "They're safe, Gareth. Listen to me, they're safe and being looked after. Sanctuary is privately owned and totally outside of the FBI. We have your family somewhere Bullen will never find them and they went of their own accord."

"How can you be sure—the FBI—" Gareth stared pointedly at Lee who didn't waver in returning the stare.

"We know there's a leak in the FBI and we have your notebook."

All the piss and vinegar left Gareth in an instant and he instead became this loose thing slumped in his seat.

"How could you do that to them? That was the only thing keeping them alive."

"No, we are keeping them safe and alive now. I have something for you." Adam pulled out a folded sheet of paper from his pocket and slid it across the table.

Lee frowned. What was this?

Gareth unfolded the sheet carefully on the table as if it may explode in his face and as he read the contents his face crumpled. An old man was sitting in the chair. A tired old man. Lee leaned in slightly and read the words upside down. The letter was signed Maggie and Josh but not much of it made sense. The page was filled with code; for all Lee knew it could be instructions on how to break out of prison. Josh had admitted his dad sometimes used a code that he had made Josh learn as a child. He suspected whatever was written there meant an awful lot to Gareth though. Gareth picked up the letter and clutched it to his chest lifting a glassy gaze to Adam. Evidently the coded letter was working.

"What do you want to know?"

Adam leaned forward with his elbows on the table and explained they had the notebook, evidence from Gregory Bullen's wife, names, dates, and photos.

"What we need is someone to stand up and testify that this all connects. A person who can join the dots and make a cohesive prosecution win this case."

"How long will you protect my family?"

"As long as they need to be. New identities, relocation, a new state and a new country if necessary. Whatever it takes to give them a completely new life."

Gareth Headley sat back in his chair.

"How can I trust you?"

"You need to trust someone," Lee said softly.

"No I don't. I can sit here in this prison and the evidence I have will sit in the bank and my family will be safe."

"Your family is only alive for as long as you are useful," Adam said. "Tell me how useful you are in prison? Tell me how useful you become when Alastair's back is against the wall and he looks for leaks in his organization."

"I'm not part of his organization," Gareth said quickly.

"But you are. Everything you did was for the Bullens. You were their bitch as much as any hired goon."

Lee looked at Adam sharply. Insulting the guy probably wasn't the best offensive to take. He turned his gaze back to Gareth who was staring at Adam in shock.

"You promise me they are safe?"

"What did the letter tell you?" Adam

asked gently.

"It said I should trust you, that Josh and Maggie are safe. That they trust you." Lee imagined there was something in the letter that confirmed to Gareth that it was indeed the work of his son and wife. Something alongside the code—maybe a memory that only they would know to share? Sadness clutched him at the thought of a family destroyed with so many memories still existing. Then he shook the emotion away. Gareth Headley had shot Elisabeth Costain in cold blood. He was a murderer. Whatever had driven him to do it he had still made that final decision to kill.

Gareth sighed. He coughed. And then he began to talk. "It started when I took money from a young Alastair Bullen to turn a blind eye on a corruption case. I needed the cash. Not long married you see, with a baby on the way and a cop's salary that barely covered food and a roof over my family's head, let alone maternity bills. I wanted more than what I had, more for my family. I would see these guys, Alastair, his brother, Gregory, in these flashy cars, tipping more at a restaurant than I earned in a week." He stopped and then shuffled in his chair so he could lean on the table for support. "I was young and so damn wrong. Hell, it was an instant of madness, but it tied me to them for twenty years or more. They had that one thing over me," he shook his head sadly. "They always said they would look out for my family. But we knew what that meant. Josh was on their radar. A clever kid. He deserved more than me as a father. Then..." Gareth's voice tailed off.

"Go on," Lee encouraged.

"They said one last job. I'd turned direction on cases the other way, passed information. Never murder. Then one last job. I wouldn't be asked anything again. If I did this then they would stop holding my son's life in front of me."

"You're referring to Elisabeth Costain," Adam confirmed.

"Yeah. They threatened Josh." He looked at Adam then Lee directly. "These aren't excuses. I know what I did was wrong. Way past wrong. I am the worst thing to happen to my family. You have to promise me. If I stand for this, for you, and give evidence against the Bullens, I don't want anything for me, I don't expect that. But you protect my family."

"You have our word," Adam said.

He wasn't sure what had been written in the letter from his wife and son, hell he wasn't even sure what tipped Gareth to talk, but suddenly everything left Gareth in a flood. There was nothing new in what he was saying but he was coherent and Lee felt a frisson of excitement that travelled his spine at the thought of what damage this man could do on the stand.

"When I looked up and saw that guy watching me, seeing me shoot that girl? I just panicked and ran after him. No one used that alley, no one was supposed to see me, and right there and then, when I couldn't find the witness, I knew it was the beginning of the end. I don't know what I would have done if I had caught up with him. Used my gun, probably. I'd gone so far down and I was spiraling out of control." He stopped and there was an expectant pause as Lee waited for more. When Gareth said nothing Adam prompted him.

"There's one last thing. You are aware someone inside the FBI is having his strings pulled by the Bullens. The initials you used in your book are SH. Do you have a full name to match those initials?" Adam asked.

Lee waited, his heart beating in his chest so loud he was worried the other two would hear.

"No," Gareth shook his head. "I know it was a guy, he was only ever referred to as 'he' and they used the initials S and H on anything they wrote. That is where I got it from. I would be 'invited' to meetings; just a subtle way to remind me of who I was I guess."

"Thank you," Lee said softly. He had expected more of a fight from Gareth. Having his family safe was clearly the catalyst and offers from the FBI for that very thing would have been wrapped in the knowledge that the Bureau was compromised. For Adam to sit here and promise something else altogether, a place outside of federal control, seemed to tick the right boxes.

When the gate shut on them and Lee finally stood outside the prison he felt the tension uncoil from his spine one inch at a time. The DA was booked to arrive shortly, everything was planned and their job here was done. Literally. Done. There was no reason for Adam to stick around now. Lee had to go back to his office and put in place something to get his head around SH and what it meant to the office. He just wasn't sure whom he could trust.

Adam pulled his cell from his pocket and connected a call as they walked back to the car. That put a stop to Lee having to find something to say as he processed everything that had happened in the prison.

"Manny," Adam paused evidently listening to the other guy. Lee took a moment to stare. They were few and far between these times when he could look at Adam without feeling like Adam was going to turn and snap at him to stop. Lee had mapped every inch of his face with kisses and loved every part of the big bear who would hold him so gently. Why hadn't he listened to his heart? Why had he immediately assumed that the man who was the other half of him was capable of doing something as out of character as compromising the job he loved?

His dad. It had to be that. Trust was so

hard to find in his family; his mom would side with her husband. She didn't have much of a hand in the child he had been, nor in the adult he had become. Hell, everything people saw now, the clothes, the education, the voice he had cultured. None of it was real but it was him. Christ. A psychologist would have a field day with him. The thought of sitting in a chair and telling someone this filled him with horror. He didn't do very well being told what to do.

"We've narrowed it down to a male voice. I need you to file a report in a couple of hours and copy the Bureau in on it by accident... Yeah." Adam chuckled. "Yeah, I know it makes you look like an idiot."

"Adam?" Lee interrupted with the question.

"Hang on a minute," he said to Lee. Then he carried on talking to Manny, "post an e-mail saying that we have a lead."

"Adam, what the fuck?"

Adam turned his back on Lee and held up a hand to forestall his questions.

"Yep," Adam was saying to Manny. "They'll know we got Gareth to agree to cooperate with the DA. That was old news as soon as I contacted the DA's office. On the copy imply only Lee and I have handwritten evidence and as soon as we're back and you have it you'll pass it over but just wanted to give them a heads-up. We're holing up. We need... yep, okay."

He ended the call. Lee waited for an explanation but he was thinking maybe he already knew.

"You're creating a trap for whoever this SH is," he stated simply.

Adam nodded. "Manny says Sanctuary three is our best bet. It's old and being decommissioned, one of the originals outside Albany. Maybe two hours out from here. We go there, we wait. We see what happens."

CHAPTER 11

Adam eyed S3 from the vantage point of his 4x4. The structure was an older building, part of a complex of smaller cabins just outside the city, and it had been deemed unusable as a safe house a while before. Nik had already been here to check on its decommission but Manny assured Adam that it was still sound. The techs had been there to rip the guts out but Manny explained how a few wires could get the thing back up MacGyver style to connect to comms. It wouldn't have been top drawer wiring but the building was not off the beaten path any more. A nearby beauty spot had been added to some kind of treasure trove hunt which left the site too close to the walkers' path. Shame really. It was a gorgeous cabin; all crooked walls and exposed wood and would have been a cool place to stay for a while.

They had chatted in the car,

inconsequential stuff between songs on the radio, and Adam was calming himself down over the whole Sean Hanson mess. Was it wrong that he wanted it to be Sean who was the mole and for Adam to have the satisfaction of shooting the guy? Just for being in Lee's life. Hell, he had it bad.

"There isn't much left here," Lee began conversationally. "It's not like the other place we stayed." Lee was crouched on the floor holding two wires while Adam tried to loosen the last wire they needed from inside the wall. Manny was adamant that they would at least get some coverage, and anyway he said he had talked to Jake who had assigned Dale and Michaela as backup. Somewhere out there in the woods Dale would very soon be lurking with the new girl, watching them. It was kind of nice that a trained SEAL had their backs. Michaela was no slouch either, an ex-cop, she was shiny bright and lethal with a knife.

"It's old stock. Been decommissioned as a place of safety."

Finally he managed to ease out the wire and gently pulled apart the wood that held it in place. It slipped out easily and he was crouched next to Lee with all three wires coming together. The warmth of Lee's thigh touched him, and the man's scent was a kick to his balls. Heat and warmth and the faint hint of the aftershave Lee had worn when they were together. Memories rushed him of cold nights and making love and early breakfasts and sex on every surface imaginable. The sadness that he had lost it all for something as stupid as not opening his mouth and defending himself was overwhelming.

"What goes where?" Lee asked curiously.

Adam checked his phone for the diagram and then more or less gave up as Lee huffed a low laugh, intervened and did the connection for him. He always had been the technical, clever one. Watching Lee's nimble fingers crossing and threading and twisting the wires together was a fascination in itself. Finally with the connections there Adam depressed his ear piece and tried a connection to Ops via the wireless. Manny answered. Jeez, the guy had his hand in pies everywhere.

"We have you," he confirmed cheerfully.

"Why are you in Ops?"

"'Cause I'm everywhere, man," Manny chuckled. "Hell, you never saw Scotty leave the transporter when Kirk was off ship did you? Anyway. Heads up, memo just left, and oops, I appear to have copied in FBI liaison and the Bureau comms section. Dale and Michaela are due with you in sixty. Go do something productive. Check in every thirty, yeah?"

"Will do." Adam looked around the abandoned house. There was no real sign that Sanctuary had been here apart from a few pieces

of furniture that looked older than the kind
Sanctuary would put in their safe houses. A
broken sofa with split cushions and a small
table. Nothing that comfortable to sit and wait
on. Lee hefted a bottle of water they had
stopped and purchased on the way down the
Interstate which Adam caught deftly. He was
also thrown some kind of pasta pot container
that Lee assured was good for him. The whole
thing looked to be about four mouthfuls and
ruefully his mind went straight to the lack of
food. His stomach rumbled dramatically as the
piss-poor excuse of lunch hit it.

"Still hungry?" Lee asked with a smirk.
Adam looked down at the pasta pot and shook
his head.

"Nah. I was so full I almost didn't finish
the pasta," he said wryly.

"So you don't want the devil's food Suzy
Qs I picked up as well?"

Adam simply held out a hand, "give."

Lee scooted away and laughed. It was a good sound. Yet another reminder of the old days. Keeping the cake and cream calories away from Adam was something Lee had grown very good at in their short relationship. They were Adam's weakness and he wanted them. Hell, Lee had better be prepared for what was going to happen if he didn't hand the damn things over.

Adam leaned over and grabbed Lee's wrist just above the hand holding the chocolate and pulled sharply. Lee and chocolate wavered and then tumbled toward Adam. Even though he knew instinctively that a lap full of Lee would lead down pathways they shouldn't be taking, Adam just caught him close.

"I was thinking," he said as he deftly pulled the now squished packet of cakes from Lee's grip.

"Don't strain yourself, big guy," Lee laughed.

"That I was sorry."

Lee stopped laughing and instead scrambled a little to get upright and astride Adam's lap.

"I'm sorry too."

"A lot of shit went down, Lee."

"It did," Lee agreed carefully.

"It didn't mean for one minute that I stopped wanting you or loving you. It's just…" Adam frowned. He couldn't word what he wanted to say. "I was too angry to see past my own stupidity at not just telling you in the first place."

Lee rested a hand on Adam's chest and pressed it against his heart. "Why didn't you?"

Jeez. That was a question and a half. Why hadn't he just turned around to his lover and said, hey, Lee, this guy says he has written evidence you are one of the bad guys and I don't believe it so let's destroy it. Easier said than done, he imagined.

"Would it make any sense if I said I was protecting you?"

The tender press of Lee's hand turned into a thump. "I'm an FBI agent with years of training and a nice line in martial arts. Tell me you didn't just say that."

"All of those things, Lee. I know that. But most of all you were mine, my lover, and I didn't want you to see what they said in there."

"What did it say?" Lee squirmed a little to get comfortable and Adam cursed that his dick was well into having Lee on his lap and a long way past being comfortable with just chatting.

"Stuff that implied you couldn't be trusted. An attached report on your dad." Adam looked at Lee steadily. If he was going to be honest he wanted to look Lee in the face.

"So whatever happened, one of us was screwed. Either you took the alleged evidence and ran with it, or I did." Lee's statement was so cold, but equally sounded so damning. "Why did you trust me so much?"

Adam paused. He had never actually questioned why he hadn't believed Lee was one of the bad guys. He was in love and he *knew*. That was it. Just because Lee's dad had died in prison serving time for a multitude of drug related crime that didn't mean that Lee had to be tarred with the same brush

"We were in a good place, you and I," Adam said simply. "We'd talked a lot about your dad, and hell, when you have a parent like him you can go one of two ways. Follow in his footsteps or go the way you did." Adam snorted a laugh. "You were the antithesis of your dad; the complete opposite to the point of OCD. I thought that destroying the crap that had been written would end the whole thing. Let's face it, I fucked it up, and I didn't say anything. So I fucked it up even more."

Lee leaned into Adam and placed the

cakes on the floor before wrapping his strong arms around him. "I think in the fucked up stakes I won the whole thing." Lee murmured this into the juncture of neck and shoulder and followed it with a gentle kiss that was nothing more than the touch of his lips on Adam's heated skin.

To have Lee so close was the stuff of dreams. How often had he wished that Lee and he were still partners in every sense of the word?

"What are you hoping happens here?" Lee asked.

Adam had to focus to hear Lee's voice clearly. Deliberately misunderstanding, he focused on the case.

"The usual. The bad guy gets pissed. Realizes no one outside of us and Headley knows about the potential meanings behind SH. Thinks that if he removes us from the equation his secret will be safe. The usual bad guy idiocy.

We are ready for him and it's all sorted. Kind of like a made for TV movie but with gay overtones."

"I meant us, you idiot." Lee lifted his head and Adam was pleased to see a smile on his friend's face. Lee was just the type to go over his decisions and beat them to death until it was just easier to shut himself away from the problem. Lee's smile meant something to Adam. He shifted a little until his back was firmly against the wall. The weight of Lee on him was both familiar and threatening to send him over the edge at the same time.

They ended up with lips only inches apart and Adam couldn't drop his gaze. Lee's eyes were the first thing that Adam admired. Of course that wasn't entirely true. Lee was incredibly fit in a wiry, sexy way and his ass was just so damn edible and his back was broad and…

Still, the startling silver-blue of Lee's

eyes was so unusual that Adam's first words outside of their training were that Lee would never be able to go undercover with eyes that beautiful. Lee had stood and stared at Adam for at least a few seconds although it had appeared longer. His response was typical Lee. Thoughtful and measured, he nodded and just said "your eyes are beautiful too". The start of a teasing, snarky relationship and some of the best sex later Adam was saying he loved Lee and Lee was smiling. A lot. And now those eyes were so close and, just like the first day they had met, Adam was lost in their depth.

He wasn't sure which one of them moved but suddenly he was deepening gentle kisses and gripping the material of Lee's shirt across his back.

Kissing was so perfect with this man; never just a means to an end but an act in itself. Beautiful and sexy with Lee's hands twisting in his hair it was every single thing Adam needed at that moment. The bad guys were miles away just learning what they needed to know, Alastair Bullen was at this moment being served and arrested, and he had Lee back. Nothing could harsh this buzz.

Lee tilted his head to deepen the kiss and his fingers massaged Adam's skull and then stopped to hold his head firmly. Breathing harshly he pulled back and Adam saw his eyelids open, the pupils at the center of the blue dilating as light flooded in. Adam leaned that little bit closer to demand more kissing but Lee interrupted the connection.

"Can you forgive what I did?" he asked. Hurriedly he added supporting evidence to what he was asking. "I want this. Us. I want you and I fucked it up so badly."

"I fucked up too," Adam offered.

"Two wrongs—" Lee began.

"We'll talk after this."

"But we're okay?" Lee asked. There was

fear in his eyes and Adam had only one thing to say.

"We're way past just being okay."

CHAPTER 12

When the shit hit the fan it was actually something of an anticlimax. Part of Lee had hoped that this time the bad guy would be clever. That for once the idea of killing the good guys was replaced by a speedy retreat from the country and a swift change in identity. Both he and Adam had their backs to the wall and Adam was connected to a guy called Dale who was observing with another Sanctuary operative, a woman called Michaela. Adam exchanged banter—he and this Dale were clearly friends. Of course there was talking to Michaela as well but Lee, damn his head, was focusing only on the spike of jealousy that appeared when Adam threw out lines like "you know what I'm like" or "I owe you dinner".

They were just killing time, chatting, shooting the breeze. Nothing that Adam and Lee hadn't done when they were in place waiting on the finale of some case. Even so, Lee allowed the jealousy to grow a little until he decided Dale was someone that needed watching.

"Okay. We have it." Adam interrupted Lee's speculation and largely ridiculous thoughts. Turning to Lee, Adam nodded. "Showtime. Five minutes out on foot. Tall guy. Brunet."

Adam stood, using the wall as support, and then held out his hand to Lee.

"Could be either," Lee noted. He took Adam's hand as help to stand.

"Who do you hope it will be?" Adam asked curiously.

Lee huffed a laugh; he didn't hope Sean Hanson, who was a colleague, was the archetypal bad guy. Then, neither did he want Simon Hatfield who, despite not being a friend, seemed like a genuine guy to be on the wrong side of the fence.

"Stupid question. I don't want it to be

either," he snapped. Adam was trying to lighten the situation but at this moment in time Lee was on edge and nothing was going to work.

Adam pulled his Sig from the holster and held it loosely at his side. Lee preferred his Glock, which was FBI issue, and he mirrored Adam's stance. Whoever was here was facing two agents with purpose.

Adam continued conversationally. "I think Jake would like it to be the liaison to Sanctuary, which would solve a lot of problems."

"Shut up, Brooke," Lee murmured. They moved back into the shadows of the cabin and waited. The person approaching wasn't exactly doing so with any amount of stealth. Almost like they wanted to be caught. Lee's heart sank when the guy finally stepped into the clearing in front of them and he realized who it was.

Sean Hanson. The Sanctuary liaison.

Fuck.

Sean was coming toward the cabin with his Glock held high and out in front of him. Adam nodded to indicate this was Lee's bag and Lee stepped out.

"Drop the weapon, Hanson," he ordered sharply. Sean stiffened in response and, for a second, they were face to face with guns drawn. The face-off lasted only a few seconds and when Adam moved out to stand next to Lee it was game over. Sean released his steel grip on his weapon and allowed it to hang loose from one finger.

"Drop the gun," Lee repeated.

With a shrug Sean did as he was instructed; the Glock landed with a satisfying thud on the dirt.

"On your knees," Adam instructed, "hands behind your neck." He moved to kick the gun away and then holstered his own weapon. He pulled ties from his pocket and maneuvered first one wrist and then the other until Sean was on his knees on the hard ground with his hands firmly together at the base of his spine.

Lee was cautious. It made no sense for Sean to show up here with no stealth and no back up. "Are you alone?" he asked brusquely.

Sean looked up at him and there were emotions flickering in his expression that didn't make any sense. Fear. Sadness. Resignation.

That was it. To all intents he simply kneeled there and looked resigned. Certainly not angry or piss-your-pants-scared at being caught. He'd seen Sean with a lot of emotions before when they shared a house. This resigned, almost blank expression, was a new one. The reaction tugged at Lee. Cautiously he stepped back from the face-to-face and caught Adam's gaze. Sean was facing one hell of a load of shit with added jail time and he was kneeling there impassively—like none of that mattered? Something wasn't right here. The niggle in his head and the thoughts that weren't quite lining up made him wary.

"Dale?" He tried to connect to their boundary guardians. Nothing. "You got Dale?" he asked Adam quickly and tapped his own ear piece.

Adam frowned but the gun on Sean was completely level and didn't waver.

"Dale?" Adam's voice was firm and quick as he attempted to contact their backup. "Michaela?"

Sean bowed his head and sighed visibly. It looked like every fiber of him was suddenly relaxed and Lee spun on his heel to face the forest where he knew Dale and Michaela were supposed to be.

"Something's not right," Lee said urgently. Deciding on the spot, Lee ran from the clearing and was up into the edge of the tree line with his gun held high and his focus one hundred percent on what the hell was going on.

He jumped logs and other remains of fallen trees, skirted bushes and hoped to hell he was heading in the right direction. Something had happened to comms and the tension inside him built to near breaking point.

Dale and Michaela weren't far ahead, and Lee's breathing was ragged from the speed he was sprinting up the hill, away from the cabin. In under a minute he was there and the scene before him was assessed and filed in seconds. Dale and Michaela were on their knees with two guns trained on them. If he had stopped to negotiate he had nothing. Whoever had weapons pointed at the Sanctuary operatives would have all the bargaining power.

Both guys looked his way but only briefly. There was enough time for Dale to lunge at the nearest gun wielding perp and dragging him down to the ground. Michaela moved but Lee was there first. With a cry he launched himself at gunman two, the arc of his own weapon wide as he angled his trajectory. He saw the startled, furious expression on guy two's face as they collided. The guy had brought his own gun around and fired it randomly. Lee felt the burn of fire as the bullet sliced through the top layers of skin in his arm up close and the smell of discharged weapon assaulted his nostrils. Cold, calm, rational moves followed and, without even using his weapon, he disarmed the guy. Michaela lunged for her weapon and held it to cover Lee as he scrambled to stand.

"What the hell?" Lee said quickly.

"Two man team here," Dale reported quickly. The ex-SEAL appeared calm but there was fire in his eyes. "Something took comms out and pulled any chances of aerial observation with it."

Lee digested the words. He knew Sanctuary had hands on some pretty cool counter-offensive kit. For two operatives to be caught like this with no backup was unexpected and a smack in the face. The debriefing on this was going to hurt. He felt sorry for the guy. This was his domain.

"You got it covered here?" Lee looked around at the local vicinity and the two men who were unarmed and kneeling just as eerily quiet as Sean. Dale nodded and Lee turned and sprinted back down the hill. He knew Adam would be okay but he wasn't prepared to just saunter down to where his partner stood. What if this was something more than just three guys with guns? His arm burned like a bitch and his chest was tight. The pain in his arm didn't matter since adrenaline was racing through his body, but the thought that he should be fitter than this passed quickly in his head.

To his relief Adam was okay. He'd pulled Sean to one side and was covering the opening with his gun drawn and intense focus on his face. "We're clear," Lee announced as he stalked over to Adam.

"What the fuck, Lee?" Adam asked and then grabbed him by his unhurt arm. "You're bleeding. I heard shots."

Lee dismissed the concern with a shrug. The burn was freaking painful, but it was nothing new, both he and Adam had been winged by gunfire in the past. At least he wasn't bleeding out or anything halfway as dramatic. His chest felt tight and breathing was hard but, hell, he'd just sprinted up and then down a hillside, not to mention he'd disarmed a bad guy.

"Just skin is all," Lee confirmed quickly and panted through a sharp, insistent pain building in his chest and shoulder. "Two more up there, your guys are okay, and we've lost comms with Sanctuary entirely."

"Our guy here is quiet," Adam said. Frowning at Lee's arm, he then pulled out his cell and waved it around for a signal. Finally it appeared, he connected, and he was talking to

Manny almost instantly. Lee didn't listen to the conversation; he just kept his wits about him and moved to stand next to Sean.

"Aren't you gonna ask me why, Lee?" Sean said softly.

Lee looked at the man whom he'd drunk beer with, watched bad films with, eaten pizza with. Something wasn't right. Sean had been the first person to give his condolences when Adam had left the Bureau. To offer his support. Sean was a good guy whom Lee had trusted. He leaned against a wooden support and inhaled mountain air, ignoring the burn in his lungs.

"Were you coerced?" Lee managed to ask. God, he hoped Sean had been made to betray the Bureau. Lee was hoping this was somehow the answer. He felt light-headed and cricked his neck to release some of the pressure at the base of his skull. The pain in his arm was getting worse. Fucking bad guys.

"No." Shit. Sean hadn't even hesitated

before saying that.

"Then tell me. Was it some greater reason, purpose or other bullshit?" Lee was forcing the words out but his tongue felt heavy in his mouth. Was he slurring?

Sean frowned and then smiled. He shrugged. "Money pays the way," he said.

Lee clearly didn't keep the disgust from showing on his face and Sean's expression hardened. He continued, "You can't tell me you never thought about turning a blind eye to some of what we see?"

Lee couldn't even bring himself to answer that one. Instead he turned his back on Sean and crossed to Adam who was finished talking to Manny.

"Manny doesn't have a reason for the blackout but comms are back now and we're clear here," Adam reported. "Manny's pissed and trying to figure out what the fuck happened."

Dale and Michaela arrived in the clearing with the two other guys in front of them stumbling forward with their hands raised. "Retrieval is coming in with cops. I'm taking Lee to the base hospital."

"I don't need a hospital," Lee responded quickly. He looked down at his hand which was curiously red and wet. Then followed up the sleeve of his soft gray jacket which was a similar color. There seemed to be one hell of a lot of blood for a grazing bullet. Dizziness poked at him and he swallowed. Just swallowing sent fire from his throat to his chest. He looked down at his front. There was blood there too. "Shit."

"Yes, shit." Adam moved to his side and gripped hard.

Lee attempted to shake him off but his movement was sluggish and the adrenaline in his body was dropping fast.

"What the hell did you do?" Adam

shouted.

"Think it's…"

"Let me see." Dale's voice. Firm, confident, kick-ass Dale was prodding him and pulling away material. "It's not his arm, Adam."

Dale's words were mixing in with Adam saying something, but he couldn't feel anything but pain radiating from his limbs. His shoulder. His chest.

"He wasn't wearing a vest. We didn't have them in the car. We should have stopped." Adam wasn't talking properly. His tone was off.

I'm fine, Lee tried to say. But hell, he was tired and nothing was coming out of his mouth.

"We can handle this. I'll wrap it tight… take his weapon."

What's wrong?

CHAPTER 13

Lee wasn't alone. He knew that because he could hear people chatting. He hurt. A lot. And people were talking over him and about him.

What the hell?

He's gonna be fine.

The bullet missed the important organs.

Damn idiot threw himself in front of a man with a freaking gun.

"I'm right here," he croaked. "Stop talking about me."

"Hey." A woman was leaning over him and she was dressed in pale green. A nurse then. "Welcome back."

"What the hell?" he managed to force out past dry lips. She placed an ice chip on his lips and he savored the sensation of the water trickling into his mouth. He looked left and right but she was the only one in the room.

"Your friends will be back in a little while."

"Friends?"

The nurse was moving around the room. She made notations on the clipboard that hung on the end of his bed and then moved over to him to pull at the covers.

"A rather nice young man with dark hair who runs a foundation or something. He and his brother, who is a doctor apparently. Caused a rumpus when the ER doc in charge of you got his marching orders and this new guy came in. Seems you are kind of special."

To Sanctuary? Lee assumed that was the foundation being referred to. He wasn't really anything to Sanctuary.

"Hey."

Lee looked up to see Jake Callahan standing in the doorway.

"How you doing?"

"Doing okay," Lee answered carefully.

Jake hovered at the doorway until he was pushed in by a shorter man with blond, curly hair and the most intense green eyes.

"Outta my way, big brother," the younger guy said. Brother? Okay, then the curly headed guy was Jake's brother? "Kayden Summers," he introduced himself. He grabbed up the notes and winked at the nurse who, flustered, backed out of the room with a promise to return with some food in a short while.

"Okay," Kayden began with a cursory glance at the notes. "Through and through but not the arm like was first reported. Your chest took the full hit." He rubbed at his own chest and winced. "Freaking hurts," he said, "you weren't wearing a vest. Idiot. But the bullet passed through and luckily missed vital organs. Nicked an artery though, so lots of blood, very exciting. You've been here thirty-six hours."

Exciting wasn't what Lee would have called it but never mind.

"We're looking at four more days in hospital and then R and R for maybe two or three weeks. Depends how much of a stubborn fucker you are. Questions?"

Lee could only think of one. "Where's Adam?"

Kayden looked to Jake for an answer to that one and Jake moved closer to the bed.

"Adam is involved in transport for Sean Hanson." Jake's voice sounded flat. "Did Sean give you any clue when you were together that he was on the payroll of the Bullens?"

"Firstly," Lee said on a cough, "we weren't 'together', and secondly, no, I didn't have any idea." He changed the subject away from the painful memories of seeing Sean on his knees in the dirt with that dead look in his eyes. "So you think it was the Bullens then?"

"Too many connections," Jake said simply. "With Gareth Headley, the information you had, and the fact it was Sean that showed up at Sanctuary three. Adam is transporting him to the Bureau. The other two guys were just paid muscle and apart from shooting you and carrying concealed we don't have an awful lot of anything useful on them."

"What's happened with Alastair Bullen?"

"The DA is pushing the case supported by evidence from Gareth Headley."

"And from Beckett," Kayden interrupted. He was smiling and Lee thought it looked ever so slightly sappy.

"And Beckett," Jake repeated.

"Two down then." The comment was the kind you made when your brain wasn't fully in gear. Looking at Jake's frown he realized he needed to qualify that statement. "The other brother. One dead, the other under arrest, but we still have the third brother. The senator."

Jake crossed his arms over his chest. "We're working on that."

"At least you get rid of your FBI

shadow," Lee said when the silence went on too long.

Jake frowned. Hell, he seemed to be doing a lot of frowning. Kayden placed a hand on his brother's arm. In reassurance? Or commiseration? Lee wasn't sure.

"Yeah, no more shadow." Jake didn't say anymore because at that moment there was a very welcome interruption.

"Is this a private party?" The familiar voice brought a smile to Lee's face and he struggled to sit up. Before he could do much damage to himself Adam was helping him and between them they actually moved pillows and the bed until finally Lee was more or less upright. Lee waited for what Adam was going to say first. He'd woken up from being unconscious and his immediate thought had been for Adam and how he felt about him. He wondered if Adam was still holding the same feelings for Lee.

"You took a bullet for one of my guys. If you ever need a job, Lee," Jake said from the doorway, "call me."

Lee glanced around Adam and both Jake and Kayden had left the room. Leaving the FBI wasn't on his to-do list but his options were good. Finally it was just him and Adam. What should he say first?

"How you doing?" Adam asked. He leaned in to steal a kiss and Lee wished for a toothbrush or mints or anything. He pulled back to see a grin and an expression of pleasure on Adam's face.

"Doing okay," Lee replied.

"Idiot. We should have stopped at the air base for vests," Adam admonished him. Lee shrugged. "We need to take better care of ourselves now that there's two of us again."

"I love you," Lee blurted out. That was probably the least romantic declaration of love that he had ever heard.

Adam chuckled and leaned in to hold him gently. "I love you too."

* * * *

Two point seven-five days of this enforced bed rest and Lee was going slowly mad. Alastair had been arrested and refused bail, Sean was in some kind of FBI lockdown, and Adam was hardly ever here. If it wasn't one thing it was another. Reports, driving, and general working with Manny on the comms problem and it seemed as if Adam was never around. Lee knew Adam wanted to be here but it wasn't helping that Lee couldn't get up and out of bed.

"Up and at 'em," Kayden said with a flourish of papers. "Let's quit this joint." He maneuvered a wheelchair to the side of the bed and Lee stubbornly pushed himself to sit upright and then to place his feet on the floor. He'd already managed to pull on sweats and a Tee like a caterpillar out of a cocoon but in reverse. A thin sheen of sweat covered his entire body and he felt like crap.

"You managed to spring me early," Lee commented on a loud exhalation of pain.

"There have to be some perks to being a doctor, yeah?"

Lee liked Kayden and his quick sense of humor. The good-looking guy was also completely in love with Beckett Jamieson, who Lee had yet to meet. To see that in another gay couple was reassuring.

"Where are you taking me?" he asked. Kayden was helping him up into the high seats of a Toyota 4x4.

"Where do you want to go?"

A bath, or a shower, clean clothes. Without hesitation he handed over his home address.

Kayden waited on him for exactly as

long as it took for Lee to get inside the house and be handed some kind of intercom thing that apparently linked directly to medical assistance if he needed it. He wouldn't need help. He just wanted to get clean and to sleep in his own bed.

* * * *

"Lee." The soft name was said into his ear and Lee batted the owner of the voice away. "Wake up, blondie."

Finally he opened his eyes and Adam was straddling him in the bed.

"How did you get in?" Lee asked curiously. Then wondered why the hell he had just asked that. Not a brilliant opening when the man he loved was in bed with him.

"I still have a key."

"No you don't. Standard procedure is that locks are changed annually. The key you may have had is way past useless." Okay so that was a bit of an exaggeration but Adam smirked down at him.

"So I broke in." He shrugged. "You gonna call the cops?"

Lee wriggled under his partner; his dick was uncomfortably hard and twisted in the covers. Which was a reminder of the fact that under the quilt he was still naked from after his shower.

"Nah, they'd just get in the way," Lee responded simply. Adam smiled that gorgeous smile of his and then pulled down the sheet that was covering Lee's chest. He frowned at the bandage.

"What did Kayden say?" Adam gestured at Lee's chest.

"You want me to quote him? He has a very odd bedside manner."

"Tell me about it. It was either that he had seen worse injuries at the company picnic or that you were being a wuss."

"Safe to say he stuck to the picnic line. Told me I'm all but healed, take it easy and I quote 'blah blah blah, etcetera etcetera'."

"Sounds like Kayden."

Adam scooted back a little and then leaned forward to capture each of Lee's nipples between his lips in turns. Lee arched and then hissed at the ache in his chest and side. Adam stopped immediately and made to climb off. Lee stopped him with an embarrassingly high squeaky noise of protest.

"I'm not sure I can stop. You sure you're up to this? How much pain do you have?" Adam asked seriously.

"No pain," Lee lied, "and I am so sure."

Adam concentrated on each nipple, sucking and biting into smooth skin. Lee imagined the small red marks of possession and it made him impossibly harder. Adam moved back up to chase a kiss and Lee whimpered into his mouth, hard against him. Orgasm was building inside Lee so damn fast just from the attention to his freaking nipples. This was ridiculous. He wanted the touching to last and he wanted it to stop. He needed to drive Adam as mad as he was with the intense longing that was inside him. The kiss turned into an exploration of the skin from Lee's chin to his throat and back up again.

"Off," Lee managed. He pulled at Adam's shirt and with hardly any interruption to the proceedings Adam had his shirt up and over his head. God, he was gorgeous. So big with a furring of dark hair on his chest and his nipples just begging to be tasted and sucked. Lee reached up and twisted his fingers into the hair between the nipples and tried to pull air into his lungs amidst the tension of pain in his shoulders.

Adam stopped and once again pulled back. Lee wanted more and he let out a whine of frustration at the pain in his body and the loss of the kiss. Adam shifted, climbing off of Lee, stripping off his jeans and boxers until he stood gloriously naked in front of a needy Lee. He seemed to be considering what to do and finally he apparently decided. With gentle care Adam maneuvered Lee until he could slide in and behind and then settled Lee between his legs. Lee relaxed against his larger than life lover and wriggled until he could feel Adam's hardness pressing against his lower back.

"Just lay still Lee, let me touch you, stay still," Adam whispered. His hands reached around and a soft touch travelled the length of Lee's body.

"Are you warm enough?" Adam asked considerately. Given he was tracing a path of heat from nipple to nipple Lee considered it a feat that he could coherently link together *yes* and *more*.

They hadn't been together in such a soft and quiet way for so long. Adam obviously wanted this to be peaceful and gentle, and he slid a hand down to wrap around Lee. Lee gasped softly, instinctively pushing his hips up under Adam's touch.

"Careful," Adam whispered.

Lee wanted to arch up into Adam's grip and cursed the pain in his body. Adam placed one hand firmly on Lee's hip, holding him down even as he began to twist and move the other hand, his thumb sliding through the clear fluid collecting at the end of Lee's dick and sweeping it down to smooth his actions.

"Should have thought of lube," he murmured. Lee mewled in his grip and arched his neck for Adam's mouth. There was no time to stop now. He was so close.

Adam didn't slow the rhythm, even as he traced each finger impression on Lee's neck with his tongue, kissing each mark. Lee tensed again faced with the decision, or the need, to run with this. Adam tightened his push on Lee's hip, using his chin to anchor at Lee's neck, whispering nothings into Lee's ear, soft meaningless words, reassuring with his touch and his voice. Finally, orgasm ripped through him and Lee arched against Adam's hold with a whimper. Adam continued to move, pushing himself closer to his own orgasm, as he supported Lee's weight. He was still whispering into his neck, just Lee's name, over and over and over and then he was coming and pushing hard against Lee one last time.

Adam grabbed his T-shirt and wiped between them and around Lee's dick and then with a sigh he pulled the quilt up and around them.

"I love you, big guy," Lee turned his head to locate Adam's lips for a kiss.

"I could get used to this," Adam said softly. "Loving you and lying in bed with you."

Lee laughed. "One thing though. Stop breaking and entering."

"I can't promise that." Adam sounded so serious.

"You know what then?" Lee smiled.

"What?"

"I'll get you a key."

THE END

SHADOW OF THE WOLF **with Diane Adams**
Shattered Secrets
Broken Memories

Available at **Love Lane Books**:

Love Is In the Hallways
Love Is In the Title

AWARDS:

Best Paranormal Author 2010
Nomination: *Love Romance Café*

Best GBLTQ Author 2010
Nomination: *Love Romance Café*

Oracle
Best Gay Paranormal / Horror 2010:
Honorable Mention (5th)
Elisa Rolle's Rainbow Awards

Oracle
Best Cover 2010: Second Place
Elisa Rolle's Rainbow Awards

Oracle
Best Cover 2010: Runner Up
Love Romance Café

The Christmas Throwaway
Top 10 Bestselling Books of 2010
Are (All Romance ebooks)

REVIEWS:

Lisa from Michele n Jeff Reviews gives 5/5 to
The Christmas Throwaway

RJ Scott has created a beautiful and inspirational story that grabs hold of the heart and doesn't let go, even after its final words are read. It is a sweetly sentimental book that cultivates an emotional response and inspires belief that love can prevail under the most improbable of circumstances. The characters are well developed and engaging, and the attraction between Zach and Ben was entirely credible. To use a trite but true cliché, The Christmas Throwaway is simply a feel-good story, a touching and romantic read that embodies the meaning of new beginnings and happy endings.

* * * *

Book Wenches give 4.5 to *Moments*

Although I began reading it looking for a Hollywood train wreck, this novel is much more than that. It is a well-told story of love, personal growth and redemption that I found to be touching and quite involving. It features well-developed and arresting characters, heartfelt emotion, and a romance that is both intriguing and affecting… I will definitely be seeking out more of Ms. Scott's work in the future.

* * * *

Readers Roundtable gives 5/5 to *Oracle*

Oracle by RJ Scott is in one word beautiful. You have to take the journey with Alex to find that beauty but it's there and it will bring a smile, and a few tears, to your face.

* * * *

Black Raven's Reviews gives 5/5 to *The Heart of Texas*

The Heart of Texas is a delightful novel with many fascinating layers. The love story between Jack and Riley is heartwarming and realistic. Their sex scenes are beautifully written, extremely erotic, and filled with emotion. RJ Scott is an immensely talented and gifted storyteller, and I highly recommend this engaging romance.

* * * *

MM Good Book Reviews gives 4/5 to *The Only Easy Day* (Sanctuary 2)

… I will recommend this to those who love danger, explosive car chases, hot sex, total alpha men, bloody rescues and a happy (for these men) ending.

* * * *

Queer Magazine Online on *Back Home*

Back Home is a really touching story that showed me the power of communication. When I started reading this story, I started having an idea about what I thought the story is about and by the end, it was a completely different picture. I love how RJ has taken on such a complex subject matter and turned it on its ear, smoothly incorporating family opinions and history to build tension and drama. Written in a contemporary style, if you enjoy drama, or family style stories, this is for you.

* * * *

Literary Nymphs gives 4/5 to *Back Home*

Back Home is another intense emotional story by author R.J. Scott that's filled with drama, pain and what it means to be part of a family.

* * * *

Night Owl Reviews gives 4.5/5 to *Guarding Morgan* (Sanctuary 1) and a 'Night Owl Top Pick Review)

I liked the premise of not only the story, but of Sanctuary as well. I found the characters likable and I liked that they were not one-dimensional.

* * * *

Queer Magazine Online on *Deefur Dog*

This is a wonderful love story which portrays that a nontraditional family has the same joys, sorrow, problems, angst, and love as any other family and does it extraordinarily well. I highly recommend it to anyone who wants a wonderful, emotional love story with a happy ending.

* * * *

Top to Bottom Reviews gives 5+ kisses to *Love Is In the Title*

RJ Scott has written an outstanding young adult story, one that can be appreciated by those who are right now living in the midst of those very trying times, as well as those who have lived through them and managed to somehow survive.

CPSIA information can be obtained at www.ICGtesting.com
Printed in the USA
LVOW131736141112

307334LV00001B/16/P